O.Z. DIGGS HIMSELF OUT

March 5., 2023

Lex,

You have now met who I always wanted to be.

Ron Baxley, Jr.

You will always be my friend. Ron Baxley Jr

O.Z. DIGGS HIMSELF OUT

ISBN: 0-9980582-5-4
ISBN-13: 978-0-9980582-5-2

Cover art by Gwendolyn Tennille
http://witchybreeze.wixsite.com/greenwitch-gallery

Cover and Interior design by Jack Gannon
www.ybrpub.com

O.Z. DIGGS HIMSELF OUT

Acknowledgements

With Great Appreciation and Thanks to Gwendolyn Tennille, who helped me "picture" Oz.

With thanks to Raymond Houck, who showed me his walking stick with the carved lion head after I told him about my Society of the Walking Cane concept for the book.

And in honor of Oz author James C. Wallace II, who shared in many memories of Oz with me.

O.Z. DIGGS HIMSELF OUT

Dedications

In memory of my late father Ronnie Rowell Baxley, Sr., who lost his completely.

In memory of my late grandmother Hattie Baxley, who partially lost her memory.

O.Z. DIGGS HIMSELF OUT

"I have seen wicked men and fools, a great many of both; and I believe they both get paid in the end; but the fools first."

--" Kidnapped"

Robert Louis Stevenson

O.Z. DIGGS HIMSELF OUT

Chapter 1

The Man with the Emerald Green Button

I HAVE ALWAYS HAD TO INTRODUCE MYSELF AS O.Z. Diggs the Seventh, and I do not mean that figuratively or merely compulsively. I have done this whenever I have met anybody in the United States in the Out World because I literally have to. They never believe I am from a family of wizards, however.

Thank goodness one of the curses of the Wicked Witch of the West on my family before she died did not require me to state the full name of my great-great-great-great grand-father every time: Oscar Zoroaster Phadrig Isaac Norman Henkel Emmannuel Ambroise Diggs, the name I share with my ancestors. I really would have been a PINHEAD had I stated that often. All I had to do was introduce myself, again, as O.Z. Diggs the Seventh, not the full name but with the new suffix.

The curse did more than this. In fact, one of the reasons my ancestor so quickly revealed to Dorothy and company exactly who he was as an old humbug did not merely have to do with Toto knocking down that Chinese screen (some think it was a curtain he pulled aside... pay no attention to that). Westy, what I call the Wicked Witch of the West, thought O.Z. Diggs the First was a charlatan. Westy knew the original wizard of Oz had sent Dorothy to defeat her. She made it so all male heirs would take on O.Z. Diggs' name and would have to be introduced by the name O.Z. Diggs and not as Oz the Great and Terrible Wizard. Old Westy could be quite the witch.

Part of Westy's curse is that once the original O.Z. Diggs traveled back to the Out World and started a family with Madame Staffia that the couple could return, but their heirs could not. At least, that is, not until the curse was broken.

O.Z. Diggs the First and Madame Staffia raised my great-great-great-grandfather until he came of age, told him the story to pass on to the next generations, and returned to Oz. My great-great-great grandfather settled in Boone, North Carolina, met a quiet, gorgeous mountain girl (in contrast to him) not far from there, and started a wood siding-covered general store which eventually became more of a souvenir store there which his son also continued with for mountain tourists. My great-great grandfather, great grandfather, grandfather, and father all also owned, worked in, and ran that tin-roofed (TIN ROOF... TINWOODMAN RUSTED...private joke) store.

The store, Nick of Time Nacks, was stuffed full of work by local artisans and North Carolina souvenirs on the wooden shelves on the creaky hard-wood floors. (Let's just say we had seen more bears of every variety than the Teddy Bear Country of Oz residents have.) Among our many preserved goods for mountain life, we had crates, barrels, and apothecary jars filled with candy of all varieties. The sweets outnumbered the wooden and plush black bears.

Eating these candies and preserved goods while we worked, in addition to Southern home cooked meals brought in while we waited on customers, kept us paunchy. Being on our feet and going back and forth with customers kept our legs relatively muscular and skinny. Like our ancestor, we had paunches but with skinny arms and slightly muscular legs. Some of us were balding like our ancestor, but I thankfully never lost my long set of curly locks. In fact, when I was a boy, female customers commented on what pretty hair I had. When I was very little, some said I looked like a girl.

With my grandfather, my father co-owned and worked in Nick of Time Nacks some but performed in his old age as the Wizard of Oz at the old Land of Oz theme-park in Beech Mountain, North Carolina about 30 miles away or so. The locals sometimes called us "Yankees" (especially quite a few years ago) or sometimes called us British but always knew our dialects were not from around there. "You ain't from around here" would be the common cry of local old-timers and even their juniors. How many times did I hear that?

Even the local artisans' hand-carved wood bears we had in our store would not convince them that we were from the area – just like the one at the Daniel Boone Inn Restaurant did not convince everybody the restaurant was truly local either. (Well, it was relatively modern, despite its antique décor, and did not date back to the time of Daniel Boone as a restaurant, yet it was local.) A waitress at the quaint, white-boarded Daniel Boone Inn restaurant did not believe either that we were originally from Boone during one of our last family gatherings there before great Grandad passed away (I was too young to know the others... just heard about them).

Before the salads with creamy home-made buttermilk ranch dressing and Southern iced sweet tea, perfectly fried chicken, salty and buttery ham biscuits with the restaurant's signature acridly sweet cherry jam on the side, and well-seasoned vegetable sides came out, we each introduced ourselves as per our norm. I will show it back-to-back: "I am O.Z. Diggs, the fourth. I am O.Z. Diggs, the fifth. I am O.Z. Diggs, the sixth. I am O.Z. Diggs, the seventh." The others' wives, and my grandmothers (save for great-great-grandmother, who had passed away) and my mother introduced themselves, quiet unassuming women who were not staunchly feminist save for my mother (I heard O.Z. Diggs the First's wife, Madame Staffia was, too). My mother, who has also since passed away, stated, "There are certain issues that keep the men having to introduce themselves first. It's hard to explain." She looked embarrassed. The waitress, a buxom Appalachian State University brunette, stated, blankly, not seeming to hear well or understand, "I am Joleen, and I will be your server. What can I get for you? Oh... by the way... where are y'all from?"

Being the patriarch, my great grandfather mumbled the answer in a tired, scratchy voice, "We're from here... from Boone."

"Get out!" said the girl who hailed from somewhere north of Charlotte. She said she lived in a dorm in nearby, sprawling Appalachian State University.

Had my ancestor heard that Out World idiom created during the years when he had been away, I imagined he would have left! He would have literally gotten out!

She continued, "I can't believe y'all are from here. You sure don't sound like it."

Many of us stared around awkwardly. Other looked at the décor as I did. On the walls above the wooden tables were quilts of many varieties, small hang-able antiques, and samplers. Antique furnishings lined the walls. It looked like the way I heard O.Z. Diggs the First had described Aunt Em Gale decorating her house in Kansas and eventual place in Oz. He heard about the former place from Dorothy. I read about it in L. Frank Baum's first book. Dorothy, in person, embellished the description even more to my ancestor as did Aunt Em when she, too, moved to Oz.

We, staring around, wanted to explain to the waitress about our names and their connection to our ancestor but couldn't. Our throats clinched. Our tongues were tied.

My great-grandfather clutched his cloth napkin tightly and started to wring it in his hands. He wrung it tightly, his eyes bulging with rage.

He stated, "Young lady, we have been in this town for generations... long before you ever got here. Just because we do not sound like a bunch of hicks does not mean that we are not a part of this place. Granted, we may seem different, but we are not obliged to say why."

"I did not mean to offend you, sir. I am so sorry. Y'all look like such nice folks."

I told her that it was okay and whispered that she had hit a bit of a sore spot in our family.

The waitress flashed a pearly-white smile at great granddad. He may have been a codger, but he responded to pretty women. His own wife, my great-great-grandmother, had passed away a few years back and was a smooth-skinned, gorgeous woman who never aged a day over 50 or 60 even in her nineties. O.Z. Diggs the Fourth was not lecherous. He just admired young female beauty from afar. He was a straight, red-blooded, hot-blooded guy. Most of our men were hot-blooded.

He softened at the waitress' smile and said, "Well, pretty young lady, I think we're going to have ourselves a good meal here. I want you to come by Nick of Time Nacks and pick yourself out something nice at a student discount, too... better than what all of you sell in your gift shop here."

With this, we all enjoyed our last meal with Great-Grandpa, most eating the country meats along with the sides ravenously as I did before I better explored the talking Oz creatures through passed-on stories and L. Frank Baum's books. I eventually became a quasi-vegetarian because of thinking of those talking animal friends of Dorothy's and other characters. I had even observed relatives killing animals on their country estates and observing the killing of them at times did not set well with me. The sight of the gushing vermillion blood and sounds of crunching bones with slick organs being removed here and there nauseate and dismay me. I have taken no issue with scaling, gutting, and cleaning of cold, dead-eyed fish in general. These I catch from a stream near my cabin in Boone. The raw smells of newly-killed mammal meat and game on the farm hit one too as much as the sadness at the death, however. Their eyes seem more soulful than the fish I have caught too. Thinking of this and talking animals in Oz turns me away from being a complete omnivore. Eating fish stops me from being a complete vegetarian or herbivore. I am a choosy bear.

Anyway, as Great-Granddad soon passed away, his last debacle with the name curse was over. But not for the rest of us, of course. Dad and

Grandpa continued to contend with it as they worked in or near Boone as I still do.

The Land of Oz theme-park where Dad once worked on Beech Mountain, though closed for most of the year now, still flourishes in small ways. The now revitalized Land of Oz theme-park atop a mountain and near a ski resort is still open for special events and boasts a rentable reproduction Dorothy house, a simulated cyclone, a funhouse version of the house after the tornado took it away, a true Yellow Brick Road, a flowery, multi-hued Munchkinland with Munchkin statues and an iridescent Glinda bubble, stops with major characters, an aviary with multi-hued bird figures, a reproduction of "Westy's" castle, and a reproduction of the Emerald City complete with even the Forbidden Fountain. When the Land of Oz theme-park closed originally (back when it not only had a ski lift but a Wizard balloon ride on said ski lift, smaller stage areas and little houses for the characters, and a stage area with a giant clock and 3-D wizard show), my father sold Nick of Time Nacks for a hefty sum and invested the money wisely. We were no Vanderbilts, but we were no Ewells either. I often joke that we are "middlin'" class.

We were able to live off of the income of the sale of Nick of Time Nacks while I pursued my storytelling at festivals and my magical birthright. However, my father started to have dementia and could not remember a lot of the stories that were passed on, and remembering the stories was left to me. My father also wandered off and was listed as a missing person for many years, but I could never find him with my magic. Yes, I have magic, yet it has not always helped me. I sunk deeper into depression at that time and my anxiety escalated about where he might be. I almost gave up.

Also, it does not help that no one ever believes any of the fantastical parts of our origins. Even Oz fans look at me side-ways when I travel from Boone to different Oz conventions and festivals as a storyteller and (they think) pretend to descend from the original O.Z. Diggs as I tell my stories aloud. I do fairly well at it.

To make ends meet, however, I also work part-time as a reporter. I cover Council meetings and features on people in small towns in North Carolina – much like L. Frank Baum, who wrote about my ancestor, did in the Dakota territories. Doing features on people is a lot like storytelling. You look for interesting details and unique statements and hone in on those. Covering Council, though, is like being stuck in a numerical country. Budgets, motions on ordinances to spend money, and other logical, numerical details are emphasized. I switch numbers in my head. I am a storyteller, not a number cruncher.

Also, every meeting, I end up making people chortle by having magically to introduce myself.

The mayor of whatever town I am in to cover will usually spit in a drawl, "We all know who you are, son."

One time, I was fumbling around with trying to write who was in attendance at the meeting and put my hand half on my heart during the pledge and forgot to remove my Fedora hat (I still have not been able to locate the magic, black top-hat of my ancestor, which I am sure would have made them whisper even more).

A Council-woman interrupted the proceedings and stated loudly in front of everybody, "You need to remove that hat in these chambers."

She also said I needed to respect the pledge. I tried to explain myself, but she relished embarrassing me because I reported on something during the last meeting that was not handled properly by the Council members.

The editors know that I do a good job with details, and they give me some lee-way at the newspaper.

During that town's next monthly Council meeting, with witchy stares in my direction, I wore my Fedora but took it off just before the meeting started.

Some gasped, and some laughed. I "took it back to Oz" for a while--figuratively.

My hair, which I had already grown out below my neck yet stuffed and hidden by me in the hat at first, was dyed by me in seven different colored stripes, red, orange, yellow, green, blue, indigo, and violet. The Rainbow spirit being, also his daughter Polychrome of Oz, and even the classic song "Somewhere Over the Rainbow" was evoked by my hair.

When confronted by the Councilwoman who had given me trouble before afterwards, I told her I would bring the ACLU and a media circus in there if she persecuted me for my "transgender issues". This was not exactly true, and there are many friends of Oz who are gay ("friends of Dorothy" is code for being gay), so I intend no disrespect to them. I just had to get back at her and found my way. And I continued to seal my reputation as an eccentric with the Oz rainbow on his head. Whether I am gay or not, I will leave it to you to decide. I consider myself to be more asexual, a quasi-eunuch – particularly as I will never be able to marry or have kids according to the witch's curse. The last fated heir will not.

By the way, the only identifying Ozian feature I wear on my standard button-up shirt at storyteller events is an emerald green button with an

O and a Z on it that could have come from anywhere really but was from Oz. My ancestor's coat, green glasses, and top-hat were scattered throughout the country by collectors or antique dealers. Even the tall white conical hat Locasta, the Good Witch of the North, had given him when he reached the level of experienced mage was for sale in some antique store somewhere too, I was sure of it. O.Z. Diggs the First had trained under Glinda, the Good Witch of the South, but had received additional training from Locasta. I need to find them, all the parts of my Wizard of Oz ancestor's attire, including his hats, to be more like him. This is my first quest.

I do have one thing from my ancestor that he passed on. Recently, I have found a way to dig myself out of this mess with it. I still have one of my great-great-great-great grandfather's staffs.

The staff was carved from a fallen oak tree in Oz and has a light golden and white swirly color to it. Carved into the handle is a Cowardly Lion head with a true cowering expression, but this is on a carved dowel between two carved brackets. If magic begins to brew from its core, the Cowardly Lion head flips, and a fully courageous roaring lion head with an open mouth full of teeth is exposed and whatever magic spell is conjured rushes from its mouth with almost scary power. At least, that is usually the way benevolent, direct magic comes from it.

Through the power of the staff, I very recently received a message about the Society of the Walking Cane. The Society of the Walking Cane appears as a seemingly innocuous band of septuagenarian retired walkers and tourers, but they are really good wizards and good witches who were forced out of Oz and are incognito. They were forced out of Oz by wicked witches and evil warlocks. Yet they also could not stay to perform magic much in

Oz because Princess Ozma made a decree that only a few such as O.Z. Diggs the First, Glinda, and herself could do magic.

In fact, a band of wicked witches and evil wizards, the same ones who drove the Society of the Walking Cane out of Oz, soon left themselves. They did not like the ban on magic either. The evil ones were known to wear black leathery robes stitched with odd symbols in red thread.

In fact, according to legend, some stated that the reason the Woozy, a bear-like creature larger than a dog composed of leathery-looking blue cubes, was a lone Woozy years ago was that the Society of the Stitches killed many Woozies to get their leathery hides. The lone Woozy, like all creatures in Oz, basically lived forever. It makes me shudder to think of such blatant murder in the relatively peaceful Oz where there is a ban on such things. The wicked witches and evil warlocks who eventually became the Society of the Stitches then supposedly dyed the Woozy hides black with walnuts in cauldrons and sewed their robes with red stitches, putting cryptic symbols on them in vermillion, strong thread as well. Some stated this was where they could keep their worst spells written on their clothing at all times, lest they forget them. Others stated they were curses for any who tried to steal the painstakingly-made leather robes. No one knew if any of this was really true. No one really knew.

Yet another legend or long-passed-on rumor was that the late Wicked Witch of the West, who had a set of black leather robes in addition to her usual set of black attire and black eyepatch, gathered together many of the bees the Woozy herd used to eat and enchanted them to work for her. Some say these are the bees the Tin Woodman and the other famous four including Dorothy encountered when they were on their way to destroy Westy. What is truth and what is fiction gets blurred along the way, however. Don't I know it?!

What is at least one truth I know now is the whereabouts of the Society of the Walking Cane and the Society of the Stitches. The Society of the Walking Cane are on their way to the Wizard of Oz Festival in Ionia, Michigan. Some have argued with me that it is just a walking group, a touring group of senior citizens who use canes and walking sticks in general to walk in different areas. But I know those are no mere canes and walking sticks. They are staffs! Staffs, I tell you! ...

The incognito walking group are walking relatively slowly from the edge of Ionia to the downtown with their disguised staffs as walking canes or walking sticks. They walk slowly at a pace comparable to many fantasy characters from many films and books do while on great quests. They are walking many miles to the downtown there where a cinema shows a wonderful version of the Oz story every year during the festival. At least one traveling vintage trailer and vintage R.V. group of wicked witches and dark wizards travels there every year to try to keep me from coming into my power (some benevolent ones in their own vintage trailer caravan attend as well... the wicked witches and dark wizards in their vintage green and brown trailers and R.V.'s have been seen in black leather robes with red stitching at times). If asked by Lurline, Fairy Creator of Oz, where they have been, the evil ones in their R.V.s and trailers would reply curtly, "Traveling the Earth." The benevolent ones in their trailers would reply, "Seeking to help others." I heard this through magical transmissions to my staff from Society of the Walking Cane members. A staff can serve as an antennae or receptor after all.

24

By the way, if people begin to recognize me as a true descendant of O.Z. Diggs, something that is more likely to happen at an Oz festival where people are knowledgeable of such things, the curse is broken. And my family can go back to Oz to help defeat other wicked witches and dark wizards left behind who have appeared to fight through the years and even defeat the ones here before doing so. The evil ones are sure to be up to some plot or other. They must be trying to keep me from being recognized. Like I said, I have attended events before. No one believed who I was.

No one has believed me, and they all think I have been reading one too many Oz books and spending way too much time as a traveling story-teller at story-telling conventions throughout the country.

But let me show you this. It will take all the courage, confidence, and energy I have. I have a long journey up ahead and do not have a wife, husband, or children (the seventh heir was, as I alluded to earlier, cursed to have none... which is why it is so crucial that I travel back to Oz... I am the last hope... there is hope in the seventh son). I have some close friends, but even they do not believe me when I tell my fantastical stories and just chalk them up to eccentricity. They think I am crazy. I am in some ways but not this one.

Back at my cabin in the modern day, I concentrate, staring out of the window at a tranquil scene in my garden. My garden has been planted with poppies, bluebells, daffodils, green clover, and petunias as well as vegetables to help sustain me. Somehow, I managed to get my grandmother's green thumb, and I don't mean one like Westy's. These floral colors reflect the colors of different color-coded regions of Oz: red, blue, green, yellow, and purple. I focus on Lurline, Queen of the Fairies. I meditate. Tranquil water flows from a stream where I had my cabin built in a valley near one of the nearby mountains. An old Southern grist mill is there with a waterwheel turning in the stream. I must make my mind absolutely still and tranquil.

Sitting on a purple ottoman before me is a copy of a graphic novel about a canine steed to the elves, a Pembroke Welsh Corgi super hero named Ziggy who rescues different characters from different fantasy worlds. For clarity while mentioning another person, I am O.Z. Diggs VII, and author Ron Baxley, Jr. may have written about me at times. Ron also imbued the character Ziggy with the love he had for a shelter adopted, emotional support dog, a very affectionate, intelligent dog. Dorothy had her Toto. Ron had his Ziggy. The Wizard, O.Z. Diggs VII, would have his own Ziggy.

The love that Ron put into that character, I will extract with magic. He made a character out of a very much alive, loving canine. I, as a wizard, will make a very much alive, loving canine out of a character. Focus... focus...

The Cowardly Lion head is turning! It's turning! ROAAAAAAAAAAAAAR!

"Harn! Harn!" commands Ziggy as he appears. A brown and white Pembroke Welsh Corgi with white markings around his head where supposedly elven stirrups and a bridle once were and a white marking upon his back where once sat an elven saddle suddenly sits before me. And this magically alive character is ready to go on an adventure.

Ziggy, the graphic novel character, can truly understand human language but can only speak canine where animals can usually speak in fantastic countries such as Wonderland or Oz. I am able to carry on some relatively one-sided conversations with him for a minute, though. I feel silly at first like somebody talking to a dog on a television sitcom. However, I know Ziggy is magical and might be able to answer me in some way. If not now, eventually...

"Ziggy, you have been around elven magic... do you think I will have enough magic in this human-made staff to make it to the upper part of the state?"

Ziggy gives a series of affirmative woofs.

I ask him if he has any magic of his own. At one point, he does have access to pixie dust in his book. He yelps a loud bark, which I suppose is a no.

Finally, I ask him if he will help me battle wicked witches and evil wizards. "RA-ROOOO!" he affirms and wags his stubby tail. Ziggy the character is indeed brave.

It will take some time after bringing the character Ziggy to life to build up enough energy to teleport further northeast in North Carolina and, when energy was built up each time, travel up where the Interstate goes to West Virginia and then on over to Virginia, Pennsylvania, and a stop off in New York before going on to Michigan.

You see...I cannot afford a plane ticket for me and a free seat for who I was going to say was an emotional support dog (more on this later). I had to tell the Wizard of Oz festival coordinator that I could not afford to come as a storyteller special guest. I needed to do this anyway, so the evil ones after my family would not know I was coming.

Even over my cellphone, I had stated, the curse of the introduction as I call it, "This is O.Z. Diggs the Seventh."

The friendly coordinator with her distinctive Midwestern dialect said, "Oh, sure, O.Z., I know who you are. You do not have to say it every time."

I gulped back tears explaining that investments were not going very well, that I have a lot of debts, and that I will not be able to go this year. I pictured her well-quaffed blonde hair and understanding eyes while I spoke with her on the phone.

She had said they were very disappointed but understood and that I was welcome anytime as I was a big draw for their event.

The Wizard of Oz Festival Ionia will not be expecting me, and I am sure the element of surprise will work in my favor. I can teleport each time to a different state but only with some hours of rest each time. And in this way, I will make it to downtown Ionia just as the Society of the Walking Cane does to help them, I am certain of it. I will arrive to help them help me so to speak.

I grab a bag that I had already packed with clothes and provisions, including some dog food, bowls, water bottle, and treats I had packed for Ziggy, who I had anticipated bringing to life for many weeks, and some non-perishable food and bottled water for me. I run out of the door with Ziggy.

Before I do, though, I rush back and grab the copy of <u>Ziggy Zig-zags the Light and Dark Fantastic</u> off of the purple ottoman.

We run toward the grist mill with the water wheel, our Southern United States equivalent of the windmill that Don Quixote and Sancho Panza chased, and cross the bridge to our journey. Hopefully, you know my seemingly impossible dream is a reality, though it seems my reality is a seemingly impossible dream. I dream it and live it.

Chapter 2
The "Airy" Dreams of Many

W<small>HEN</small> I <small>AM WELL RESTED,</small> I <small>USE THE</small> teleport abilities of the "Sirius Argentum" spell, or Silver Dog. Granted, a certain bus line is sometimes called the Silver Dog, but I will let you think what you will, whether my trip was magic or "real." I sometimes imagine things so vividly in my imagination that they are truly real to me, that I can live in those realities. They are not true hallucinations as I know they are not truly real, but they are quasi-real, hazily other-worldly. Creativity makes me imagine. Magic makes imagined musings real and possible.

Through "Sirius Argentum", Ziggy and I arrive at the small downtown of quaint Mt. Airy, North Carolina during Mayberry Days, a festival which celebrates "The Andy Griffith Show". My father, even with his dementia, loved that show, something about it piqued his memory of being in a small Southern town most of his life. Crowds of hundreds, local yokels and in-state and out-of-state scholars alike, circulate in the downtown there. We pass by a colorful mural on an old red brick building of all of the locations that served as settings for the show, including Snappy Lunch, the Police Station, and others, and make our way past Floyd's barbershop with its classic barber-chair and simple furnishings to cross the street to an antique store. Many people have crowded around the Floyd Barbershop location and barber's pole to take pictures of each other and selfies, so it is hard to get through. The spinning red and white stripes of the pole reminds me of the swirling magic around magic staffs at times. We ignore the throngs of people, and I take Ziggy carefully across the street on his leash to the antique store. Many people are crossing, so it is easier.

An entire redneck family is having their family reunion there in Mt. Airy during Mayberry Days, and they each have T-shirts with the label, "We're Goobers for Goober. Golly, though, we're the Gomers. Mt. Airy Days 2016." Their last name was Gomer and matched the first name of the famous mechanic character. They have images of goobers or peanuts on their shirts to drive home the first point and a caricature of Gomer to drive home the second one of their T-shirt captions. They, truly looking like goobers, though, all have to-go country greasy spoon plates and are eating them in rocking chairs outside the antique store. The rocking chairs rock forward, blocking Ziggy and me from getting in.

I introduce myself as always, "I am O.Z. Diggs the Seventh."

"And I'm Forrest... Forrest Gump," one of the oldest rednecks with more like a business district appearance in the front and a frat party hair-style in the back smarts off. He has an ultra-mullet.

I state, getting my temper up, "You could really use some manners, you know."

Some of his sun-burned, dirty kids smack grease off their fingers and blurt, fried food being exposed in their mouths full of bad teeth, "You sure as hell ain't going to be the one to teach them to 'em."

The Gomers are blocking my way into the antique store with their many chairs. I am getting very incensed. This type of hot rage was not good. It could create focus for magic, but the magic would be diffused.

Ziggy warns me in a strange clipped bark, "Harn. Harn." He knows my magic could come from rage, and this is not a good thing. He knows from his elven masters that magic should only come out of tranquility, out of calm. He whines. His high-pitched puppy-esque whines seem to indicate that my magic should come from caring, from wanting to do good, to make a difference in the world. He whines and does a not-startling woof. Ziggy tries to gain my attention. He does not want to do a large bark to startle me. Ziggy does want my attention, though. He wants me to calm down. It is too late.

The Cowardly Lion's head on the staff stays in the position of cowardice. My actions are cowardly. Energy builds up, but it does not come from the mouth or a roar but from the eyes, from eyes that burn with rage while a scared expression still graces his face. These burning eyes on my staff shoot out red at each of the Gomers. It evokes passive aggressiveness. I glare at people like this when I am pissed too. A friend called it laser eyes.

"It's time to take you to school... to an old school... think of the one room schoolhouse my ancestor told me about... now repeat after me... G-OLLEEEEE a hundred times just like writing lines after class!" I state as the beams burn toward them. "Now rock nonchalant and continue to be as rude as can be," I end.

The Gomers, magically controlled, rock their rocking chairs clear down a block kicking them forward with their feet, screaming, "G-O-LLEEEEEE!" They must continue to do this one hundred times while I am in the store, and I know they will not mess with me anymore. The smart-mouthed kids and even Mr. Mullet have started crying. I feel badly but most move on. A spell casted in rage must go on until its finish.

I take Ziggy into the antique store. I have a letter from a psychiatrist stating that I can have an emotional support dog with me. I have failed to mention that a recent traumatic experience for me was losing my own Cairn terrier, Toto, who was an emotional support dog for me and knew when I was getting very depressed or manic. The emotional support dog letter does not specify the name of the dog, so I hope to use it. The law varies from state to state on this. Some places allow emotional support dogs in like service dogs. Others do not.

The old codger store owner, a man so leathery and wrinkled he looks like walking, sculpted beef jerky, does not mind. He has been reading an antiques journal and has not paid attention to anything that has transpired outside. As required and forced by Westy's curse, I state, "I am O.Z. Diggs the Seventh."

"Heck of a name" the old codger spits out of a mouth missing a few teeth into a nearby trashcan, "Say... there's an old book around here somewhere... nah..."

"Yes... go on ... go on..." I state. Part of my curse is that I cannot coax people entirely toward the answer.

The codger says, "Nah... I can't remember. Just help yourself. Look around and let me know if there is anything you want."

I shrug. Part of the curse is that I cannot force the answer. I rummage through the items. I even see some of the M.G.M. Oz merchandise, including some Barbies dressed as the Famous Four Oz characters as well as some little Oz nick-knacks. I even see some mugs with the old Land of Oz theme-park logo on them as well as some collector plates. Among some books, I spot a First Edition of L. Frank Baum's The Wonderful Wizard of Oz which the owner was alluding to but could not connect me to, and I would snatch it up if I had had the cash for it. I cannot duplicate cash with magic... not yet.

Ziggy yips at some stuffed animals and wants to take one, a lion cub, as his toy. I tell him to sit and behave, and he does. He even stops doing his puppy-esque whining. His pointy ears droop a little. He looks at me with wide, brown eyes.

I hate to see him so sad. There is a reason I do not want him to have the lion cub. I think it is reminiscent of the Cowardly Lion when he truly had cowardice. I would rather him have a representation of the Cowardly Lion when he is brave. Instead, I find Ziggy a left-over stuffed elf from Christmas. He gingerly carries this around affectionately in his mouth by the scruff of its neck like he would a puppy since he has no saddle for the elf to ride upon. I pay the man for it and continue looking.

Antiquated toys, antique furniture, lunch boxes, old tools, house-wares, glassware, and other items are in abundance and are sorted, categorized, and priced on different old tables here and there. However, the general appearance of the antique store, as in many antique stores, is chaotic. It appears as the proverbial organized chaos.

Andy Griffith Show lunchboxes, glasses, premiums, autographed black and white and a few signed color photographs of the cast members, small metal toy car duplicates of the classic 60s cars from the show, Opie-related children's items, and a plethora of Mayberry-themed items are all of the place and are featured more prominently throughout (they have been in the window display too). It's just that the Oz items gain my attention first. Besides, I am on the proverbial warpath for something.

Just when I think I will not find them, I do. There they are on a table with a few pairs other shades including some tortoise shell aviator glasses. The Victorian ones are what I am after, though. The Victorian glasses have copper frames with round green lenses, the glasses like what my ancestor had people wear in the Emerald City to make things appear green. They have those thin shepherd-crook like parts that fully encircle the backs of the ears. Thank goodness some of the steampunk con folks have not bought them. I buy the pair of them and put them on in the hopes that somebody will recognize me. Before I can leave and after I pay, though, three googly-eyed Barney Fife re-enactors come in to the store. They shuffle around in character, looking around the store with suspicion emanating from their eyes.

One sniffs, jerks his reproduction police cap back, lifts his fake gun-belt, and states, "You and that dog need to get out of here!"

"Yes", yell the other two re-enactors in that over-excitable squeaky drawl, "Out of here!"

I have the support dog letter, albeit one I am feigning being for another dog, but do not want to cause a stink, so I gladly comply.

The Barneys take long sniffs of satisfaction, lift their gun belts, and say things in concurrence like, "Yep. Yep. Yep. I guess we showed him."

Outside, I notice the Gomers' magical discipline is over, and they have scattered from the area, leaving their rocking chairs behind and soiled plastic plate and utensil litter behind. The rocking chairs have stopped rocking on their own volition from my temper-infused magic. It is time to get rid up the white trash from the white trash. I clean up the Gomers' mess and throw it away in the next trashcan that I see.

On the sidewalk, I make my way down to Aunt Bee's Restaurant. Funny, I do not think Aunt Bee's is supposed to be located right there in downtown. "Snappy Lunch," the place the characters often visited is downtown and is reproduced there somewhere. But I heard Aunt Bee's is not there in downtown Airy.

However, here Aunt Bee's is. There in a font that resembles an old-timey stitched sampler right in front of me are the giant letter's "Aunt Bee's Restaurant."

The store's front window displays have covered cherry pies faced out on baker's stands so that it looks like plastic wrapped covered crusty circles, dripping a little with red through tiny gashes seen in the flaky fronts, compose the front walls themselves when seen through the crystalline windows. Because of the windows and about 200 faced out pies on six baker stands, the front looks to be composed of a cherry pie pattern. It is like a modern-day Hansel and Gretel gingerbread house enticement for me – only with pie. And I love cherry pie!

When I walk in, I see that the back kitchen is exposed to the patrons and a gigantic pie oven that a seven-foot-tall man could have walked into, is piping hot and expels the most glorious sweet smells. Other than the aforementioned and the tables, the only other thing in the place is a wooden coatrack near the door with what looks like a black leather jacket with red stitching on it that somebody, probably a motorcyclist, has left behind. I think nothing of it at the time.

At the non-descript table I choose to sit at, a woman who looks like Aunt Bee, both cook and waitress with a big stained apron but her hair in a silver bun, takes my order. She, probably another re-enactor but one throughout the year, has a portly face and a plastered-on amiable smile. She also speaks in that sort of falsetto Eleanor Roosevelt-esque voice that the original actress gave the character with a bit of a twang (I have heard recordings of both). There is also a kind of non-dialect under-pinning her voice. I cannot put my finger on it. She is probably just well-travelled or went to university with a diverse multi-regional crowd. Like of my family, the locals would say, "She ain't from around here."

"Aunt Bee" does not say anything about the Corgi. Usually emotional support dogs (especially ones that one was using an old letter from another dog for), unlike service dogs, are not allowed into restaurants. Another strange thing is that it is lunchtime, there are crowds outside (who could not be seen while inside because of the blocking baker's racks), but Ziggy and I are the only ones in the restaurant. Save for us and the re-enactor waitress, it is abandoned.

Under the curse, I have to introduce myself almost immediately.

"And I am Aunt Bee," she says, "Sheriff Andy Taylor's aunt... what delicio-o-o-us goodies can I get for you today?"

(I note the irony here. Here I am an heir to a famous yet alive character and state my name without recognition from folks, but "Aunt Bee" here is not really the character she portrays and states her name probably with instant recognition from most.

If I just called myself the Wizard of Oz or Oz the Great and Terrible or a descendant of him, I would not have that problem. You know why I can't.)

When "Aunt Bee" is taking my order, I do notice that she has way too much pancake makeup on. She is much, much older than the Aunt Bee from the show but is chubby, so the age does not show as much. Looking around her eyes, I notice a near-deadness there and more like ravens' feet rather than crows', hard to cover up with makeup. (Her ravens' feet could make her dark eyes quote, "Nevermore.") She had stared intently at me when I said my name. Her eyes look truly ancient. The skin on her hands, though well-lotioned, looks very dry despite being on sausage-like fingers. She keeps a glass of water at an arm's distance walking it carefully to the table like a younger version of herself must have carried a book on her head to practice poise, I suppose. Yet I cannot be sure.

Glancing at her true self beneath her make-up, I am not even sure she ever was a young version of herself or, if she was, it was over 70 decades ago gauging her true age. She gingerly continues carrying the water before gently placing it on the far side of my table opposite where she is standing. She looks at me expectantly.

I say, after glancing over menu which had a sewn sampler appearance like the sign outside, "I will have a Kansas City-style grill with all the fixings. Skip the meat, though." The Aunt Bee waitress rolls her eyes slightly and decides not to argue. I should have just stated that I wanted pancakes and eggs. My ancestor has passed down that one of his favorite meals is a big country Kansas breakfast from Aunt Em, and I cannot disagree with him there. (Kansas City, Missouri claims it, but Kansas state house-wives made it for decades.) Pancakes and eggs are definitely comfort foods for me, and with this dish, they are cooked on the same grill or large pan with the salty bacon and/or sausage being cooked first and the grease from it being used for the other breakfast items according to some recipes. I am not so much of a vegetarian that I will not forbid her not to cook in the animal fat that she already has. However, I have grown to think of the truly alive talking animals of Oz more and have stopped eating sausage and bacon. Now, I just eat the pancakes and eggs and gladly tell faux Aunt Bee all about it. I am a quasi-vegetarian most of the time now. But not vegan.

"Oooooh, won't you take some cherry pie too with coffee afterward?" faux Aunt Bee asks.

"I don't know. I—"

"Come... let me show you where I bake them," she gushes, her voice cracking ever so slightly into an elderly wheeze.

"I would rather just sit here... I am kind of tired."

She, ever the gauche hostess even in the show, grabs me by the sleeve.

"Oh, alright," I say. I grab my Cowardly Lion staff before traveling to the back of the restaurant with Ziggy.

She takes me to show me the cherry pie oven. I had seen that she had taken out a rack with one pie on it earlier. When she opens up the over seven-foot-tall Hades-hot oven, I notice there are no other racks in it. It resembles a walk-in freezer at this point – only at the opposite end of the temperature spectrum.

When I walk just behind faux Aunt Bee, my Cowardly Lion staff drops slightly and passes over her. Her true identity is revealed as one of the wicked witches of Oz. She could not completely disguise her dry skin back at the table, and she appears as even more of a rotten green-fleshed hag through the revealing magic of the staff. She is revealed to be a chubby witch in the face as Ozian Mombi is sometimes depicted but with a green skin tone indicating years past rigor mortis yet still living, breathing flesh kept alive by dark magic. (Through my green glasses, her skin looks even greener than the green of other things seen through them, and I lift the shades just to be sure her skin is actually green through the revelation of the staff. The faux Aunt Bee witch is truly a portly green hag.) She, the dried-out, rotted hag, cannot tell I have seen through her disguise through magic. –Lucky for me.

She tugs at my sleeve hard when we got to the oven, staring at my green glasses but never saying if she recognizes me. She and other Ozian witches and wizards who have been living here a while now count as Out World-ians and can break the curse if they state out loud that they recognize me. She knows better than to end the curse that way.

The modern-day Hansel and Gretel witch had me at pie. This was the bait that brought me in and brought me to the back of the restaurant. I might, loving sweets, have even said, "You had me at Jell-O."

Ziggy tugs at faux Aunt Bee's black and white floral dress. He nudges her away from me with his strong snout. He usually licks people – especially those he loves – but averts his snout from the faux Aunt Bee witch after nudging her. He quickly scatters away on stubby legs, though, being wise enough to stay away from the open oven. Plus, he continues to avert his snout from her, not wanting to smell the disguised hag.

Before faux Aunt Bee can thrust me into the oven (the warning signs of who she is and that she has planned to kill me were all there), with my Cowardly Lion staff at the ready for extra magical power, I shove her in as a form of self-defense, slam the door, ignore the screaming, and run out with Ziggy. I felt I had no choice. I felt she was going to kill me... and my little Corgi too.

When I step out of the restaurant, I notice it is a dusty, abandoned building that had once been a mom and pop restaurant years ago. The entire restaurant had been an illusion, but the antiquated oven in the back had been real, had been re-started with magic, and could have killed me. The oven is currently killing the faux Aunt Bee, one of the disguised wicked witches of Oz. I can hear her screams but for a moment and then silence. I shudder. One does not like death in Oz or in the outside, but when a truly evil witch tries to kill one, one tries to defend one's self. I had to kill her or be killed.

That was definitely an illusory Aunt Bee restaurant. The real Aunt Bee's is now located by the mall, I soon learn from some locals walking down the sidewalk. In an alley, I use the Cowardly Lion staff to transport Ziggy and me there to the brick building about a block from the mall.

The real Aunt Bee's looks like a blue-checked, typical fast food place, has a blue unassuming sign and plenty of trucks and cars are parked in its somewhat cracked, aging parking lot. I take a deep breath and pause for a while to contemplate about all that just happened. I must move forward, though, on my journey.

I go there and grab a slaw sandwich and home-made potato chips from the drive-thru. (They do not seem to mind me walking up to me without a car as this seems to be a common occurrence.) North Carolinians love slaw on their barbecue sandwiches, but I do not want the pork. Again, I am staying away from meat as a tribute to the animals of Oz and to forget the killing of animals on family farms. From my ancestor, I have inherited a sweet tooth (I hear he loved Emerald City lime-aid with extra sugar and had to resist eating the alive treats of Bunbury) and down all of this with a Cheer-wine with a new Krispy Kreme flavor additive and a chocolate shake for dessert. The "real" Aunt Bee's had a host of desserts there. Thank God I am not a diabetic.

For some odd reason, though, I am put off cherry pie.

Chapter 3

He Thought He was Born a Coal Miner's Son

THE COWARDLY LION STAFF NEXT TAKES Ziggy and me to a cabin in a holler near some mountains in coal-mining country in West Virginia.

I do not recognize the cabin, but when the grey-bearded fellow, looking a lot like Rip Van Winkle, opens the door, I would have known him anywhere. The bright hazel eyes, the smile, the warmth that exuded from him... father!

I grab him and hug him tightly and immediately start weeping. He cries too but more in response to my crying.

He knows who I am and knows I am his son, which is good, but he has forgotten who he is entirely. He has wandered here while traveling and begging as a hitchhiker, and some neighbors have helped him build his cabin. He forgot about me for a long time because of the dementia but seeing me in person triggered his memory. It turned out, according to what he said, he told his neighbors his father was a coal miner in the area and that he had lost him years ago and had just been wandering around ever since. The neighbors felt sorry for him.

He has planted himself a garden and has some chickens for eggs and an occasional chicken meal (my father has not become a vegetarian like me).

Father, O.Z. Diggs the Sixth, says, "I am O.Z. Diggs the Sixth... please come in and sit down." He remembers to do this because of the old curse.

Ever adhering to Westy's curse, I offer my name in reply.

We sit by a fireplace, and I know not to argue too much with Dad as he is a dementia patient. I am to humor him. He will probably tell me stories about being a coal miner's son momentarily.

Ziggy sniffs around here and there in the cabin and does what I call a circus dog routine on his hind legs to try to get to a hambone drying out on a butcher block in the kitchen. I had smelled its greasy aroma which was coupled with the odor of sap in some of the logs when I came in.

"Off! Leave it!" I yell. And Ziggy descends and goes sniffing around other areas of the cabin. I knew his character had been trained by the elves.

My father points to his mantle-piece where there is a metal miner's helmet with a flashlight front on it and a clock with what appears to be a still Kabumpo the Elephant of Oz but with painted-on fine silks and encircled in his trunk that he raised above himself was a Tik-Tok robotic man with a time-piece in his front. Now, he really was ticking and tocking!

Dad explains that the miner's helmet was his Dad's, a coal miner's. He states the clock was Victorian and had been passed down from generation to generation. I know for a fact that was one of the tricky unintentional lies of dementia. That clock has never been in our house before. The rest was pretty obvious too.

Sincerely bless the elephant's and robot's hearts, though. They must have been turned into nick-knacks by Ruggedo the Nome King!

I knew Dad must have used the miner helmet to travel underground almost to Oz via some tunnels the Nomes had been digging to try to come to the United States. Because of the curse, he would not have been able to travel all the way to Oz in those tunnels. I wave my staff over the miner helmet and the Kabumpo the Elephant with Tik-Tok time-piece. All is revealed before us in a hazy vision...

Dad battled them with his own magic in those tunnels while his own great-great-great grandfather battled from the Oz side. Great great-great-great Grandfather O.Z. Diggs, who has lived eternally in Oz, was having difficulty getting magic into the tunnel because wicked witches and wizards that had arisen in Oz were blocking him. The tunnels were huge, and vast armies of Nomes were placed into them. Kabumpo had been called for from a distant land, and he had Billina, the hen, on his back along with Tik-Tok. He had managed to barge his way through into the tunnel past the Nome guards. Billina, sitting upon some of his fine silks on his back, supplied the large elephant with eggs which he would shoot out of his trunk at the Nomes to destroy them. (My ancestor probably placed a spell on the Kansas hen sojourner to Oz so that she would produce a ton more eggs just as he was good at reproducing piglets from thin air. They were shot like mortar shells out of Kabumpo's trunk but struck the Nomes like grenades and even had dangerous eggy shrapnel for the underground creatures when they broke on them or near them. They were left with egg on their faces.)

Nomes, as you know, hate eggs as they are poison to them. An eggy, shelly mess littered the tunnels as did downed Nomes. However, Ruggedo, incensed at his jewel placing and mining Nomes being defeated in such numbers, used his own staff set upon his bulbous stomach and sent a blast toward Kabumpo. Tik-Tok, who was also in the battle as the Royal Army of Oz, rushed to try to grab the staff from Ruggedo and put himself in the way of harm to protect the others. However, the blast caught both Kabumpo and Tik-Tok together. It hit Tik-Tok and continued to Kabumpo and merged them into one decorative clock. Dad had picked it up and put it in his bag, so he could help the talking elephant and robotic soldier eventually.

Blasts came from the Oz end of the tunnel, but they were too little too late in some ways. However, they kept Ruggedo from continuing.

Father had already wandered to another state with dementia. Ruggedo partially wiped more of my father's memory with temporary yet long-lasting magic and teleported him. Ruggedo screamed and vowed, tugging on his long beard, "I will be back in these tunnels again. I will re-dig if I have to! America and its stolen jewels and potential jewels will be mine! Also, I have bigger fish to fry!"

Ruggedo had meant bigger fish to fry than my father and probably not even me in the United States in the Out World, but I was not sure who he meant, who he was after. The rest just sounded like typical Ruggedo behavior. However, the wicked witches and evil warlocks in red-stitched leather robes who were left behind by the others of their group were starting to rise up in Oz and use magic against the wishes of Princess Ozma, who had banned it from most. They must have helped Ruggedo more than just in numbers and keeping my ancestor and his heroic friends out of his giant tunnel. The Society of the Stitches must have combined their powers to remedy the last time Ruggedo had drunk from the Forbidden Fountain. Another Nome ruler had taken over since then, but Ruggedo, upon re-gaining his memory thanks to the evil ones, must have led a coup. (And not a chicken "coop" either.)

The vision is gone as are my thoughts for it for now, and we all see the threadbare main room of the cabin again. Ziggy is off in some back room sniffing around, but I do not have time to call him. This situation is urgent.

Quickly, I grab the elephant clock with the Tik-Tok time-piece off of Dad's stone mantle-piece.

"Hey... be careful with that! It's a priceless family heirloom!" Dad screams, chasing me out into the front yard.

Using my staff, I do a reverse magic spell on the nick-knack. Suddenly, Kabumpo and Tik-Tok appear.

I say, "There is no time to lose. Take the tunnels back to Oz and help continue to fight the Nomes."

"Yes, Your Majesty... I would have expected you in finery more like mine, but we will help you," says Kabumpo.

Tik-Tok states, "We-will-help-where-we-can." Kabumpo trumpets a loud elephant cry, and I try to shush him. He is heading out quickly, though, so I am not too worried. The characters, even the majestic elephant from another country who chooses to, have allegiance to Princess Ozma, by the way, yet still respect the legacy of Wizards. Tik-Tok tells me that he will procure my ancestor's black bag for him which he has left behind in a rush. I shake my head yes but also shake my head back and forth in general disappointment. The recognition by "In World" inhabitants does not break Westy's curse.

Tik-Tok soon jumps on the elephant's back, and he stampedes off to one of the old coal mining tunnels which eventually connected to the Nome's tunnel.

Seeing all this, Dad says, "I am O.Z. Diggs the Sixth, and there is a magical legacy in Oz!" Through my magic staff, he has seen the vision of what transpired in Ruggedo's tunnel too. He remembers! He cannot say our connection to it. He is cursed not to be able to. Yet he can state there is a magical legacy itself and remembers. I rejoice!

I hug Dad again and laugh with joy. The magic and the memories have jarred something in his mind. Connections have been re-forged.

Suddenly, from where he had been rummaging, Ziggy comes out of the open front door and brings out a black, magic hat in his mouth. He has clamped in it his mouth via the brim.

He drops it at my feet. I grab it, remove my Fedora I mentioned wearing to meetings and everywhere and put it away in my bag, and don the black top-hat over my long, rainbow-colored locks which jut out a little from its back brim.

"Good boy, Ziggy. Dad, I've got to go. I've got to make everything right. Go back to Boone at my place... you may be safer there as the villains in Oz think you're here now. You remember where that is, right?"

My father nods, chewing on the part of his beard just around his mouth in thought.

"Son, you truly are going to be the heir to make everything right again, aren't you?" He cannot say exactly who I will be in Oz, what title I will have there. Others will have to do that to break the spell. -Part of the curse.

I nod, adjust the top-hat on my head, and stare at him with the green glasses. Dad thinks to himself for a minute. Things are still coming a little slowly for him.

"Now there's an O.Z. Diggs who is looking more and more like, well, you know," Dad exclaims and pats me on the back. He gives me a big hug, and I return it. I give him some money (enough for a bus ticket and a meal and a bit of a role reversal) and tell him I will check in on him via the land line when we both get further down the road. If only the United States had the easy to navigate Yellow Brick Road... I-95 was close to it, but I was led to stop-offs by the lion staff that did not require I-95.

Interrupting this thought, my father suddenly states, "Say hello to the reincarnated spirit of Mombi when you see her."

I shrug and ask, "Huh?"

O.Z. Diggs VI does not reveal a lot more, but I will have to find out more later. He has just gained a good bit of his memory back, but it will take time to gain the finer points back. What he remembers is hazy at best and probably inaccurate.

O.Z. Diggs VI, my grey-bearded father, states, "That's all I can remember for now. Good luck and safe journey, my boy."

We hug once more. Love and good magic motivate us, motivate our family.

I suddenly realize that despite feeling good about being loved and having access to good magic that I am still exhausted and hungry.

We sit down and eat some salads from Dad's vegetable garden because I have to work up more energy for the trip and the magic I will have to use to teleport to Pennsylvania (I am going to skip over Virginia, I have decided). Ziggy is treated to some cut-up ham from that bone he was eyeing earlier mixed in with some of the dog food I brought him. Even brought to life fictional characters have to eat.

Dad and I talk about the old days and our ancestor over dinner, and even more starts coming back to Dad about how we ended up in Boone, Nick of Time Nacks, the Land of Oz theme-park, and his own childhood memories on forward.

We even bring up the time as a teenager that I wanted to deny my magical heritage. I was going only to be a storyteller, which I still am, and work in Nick of Time Nacks. I was against Dad selling it for many years. I had a captive audience within the general store turned souvenir shop. When people would come in Nick of Times Nacks, they would gather around me and listen to my stories. They would sit on decorative barrels and make-shift log furniture. Folks from all over were entranced.

Dad states, remembering this, "You were like your great granddaddy when he used to sell produce at the farmer's market in addition to selling at the store. He always did have a small crowd around him listening to his stories."

There were keys to unlocking people's interest in orated stories, particularly local ones, and I found them at an early age. They had to have a supernatural hook (some Appalachian ghost, for example), begin in medias mess (not in medias res, the middle of things, but media mess, a problem of epic proportion), had to have end of your seat suspense, humor, and a twist ending that sometimes left people hanging. This kept people coming back for more.

Anyway, Dad states he remembers how good I was at this, but this did not stop him from secretly trying to get me to fulfill my magical legacy back then. He introduced me to my ancestor's Cowardly

Lion staff and showed me the rudimentary aspects of concentration and magic with it.

Dad wanted to keep the magic alive by continuing to play O.Z. Diggs at the local theme-park and wanted to sell the store so that I could continue to pursue my magical legacy. I pursued being a storyteller more often.

Dad stated at the time, "Now you listen here, and you listen good... this family has worked hard to keep the magic going through the years. I do not want to see you throwing all that way by being some threadbare storyteller."

He was right, of course. I had to supplement my income as a storyteller by being a reporter eventually. Thankfully, he had sold the store anyway because we needed to live off of that investment money.

Dad says in the modern day, "I am so glad that you decided to pursue the true family business, magic."

I nod. I state, "I'm just glad I stopped all that storytelling I was doing in my twenties when I was making you out to be a villainous king banning the medieval minstrel from telling his tales... I used to tell that one at the Renaissance fair if you remember. Now I focus on more positive storytelling."

"Teens and people in their twenties ain't fit (he slipped into local dialect at times too) for society yet. They have not been through enough to realize what they are complaining about really isn't that bad," he states, stroking his earned white beard.

I para-phrase a quote from Mark Twain, a quote which changes just about every time I see it, "When I was 18, I thought my old man was the dumbest man in the world. When I turned 19, I learned how much the old boy had learned."

We have not always been affectionate, but I give Dad a big hug after saying this, and the corners of his moustache lift up, and his beard does a little as well. He has had some dental issues, so he is missing one or two teeth but not in that exaggerated hillbilly dental stereotype. The couple of missing teeth give his smile character, and I have joked with him that he has a Jack O'Lantern grin.

"Okay, Jack Pumpkinhead, I have got to get out of here soon," I tease. I had to learn years ago that a little teasing was how Dad conveyed his affection.

"Alright, Cheshire Cat," he teases back. I have a big Cheshire Cat yet close-mouthed grin in his direction. I tend to do a big grin as I do not like to show my slightly yellowy teeth. My mom always said Scots-Irish folks bear the brunt of the curse of soft teeth. Well, my teeth are not the best in the world – just like my father's.

Dad is remembering more and more now that memories from Boone and magical memories from Oz have been brought up. For some reason, I was able to tell the inhabitants of Oz and the distant magic land who I was really. For a while, I had heard I would not even be able to tell "In World" Oz residents when I met them. Perhaps the curse is starting to wane. Perhaps the Nome King's spell over my father has completely weakened as well.

Once I am re-energized and say my good-byes to Dad once again, I use the Cowardly Lion staff to blast Ziggy and me on to an unknown destination in Pennsylvania. I hope it will be Hershey. I probably will not be that lucky.

Chapter 4
Virginia is for Elf Lovers

I AM NOT THAT LUCKY. I DO NOT HAVE ENOUGH magical power built up to make it to Pennsylvania. We end up at a restaurant property with a For Sale sign on it some distance from the Interstate in Virginia.

The restaurant has a trapezoidal roof and a big yellow sign outside which reads partially in Appalachian hillbilly slang, "The 'ELFFAW Hut: Guaranteed to be the Most 'ELFFAW' in Town." A mirrored mini-skyscraper, also for sale, reflected the letters, and I saw that ELFFAW was also backwards for "WAFFLE", though I did not know if that was intentional or not. I also saw that the owner had chosen to use the strategy of a peanut business in Columbia, South Carolina. Once, someone had bad-mouthed said business stating that they had the worst peanuts in the city. The peanut business owner decided to put on his sign that his peanuts were the worst in town. Then, people started flocking there to see just how bad they were. Perhaps that was the strategy here. However, it must not have worked because the restaurant was closed, and the building was being sold.

Ziggy sniffed near a dumpster that I pulled him away from. The restaurant had been closed so long that the dumpster looked almost clean. It was not hard to get Ziggy away from it as no enticing, putrid smells for canines were there. Anyway, as per the restaurant closing, Virginia, at times, is just Southern enough to have such a business like a Southern greasy spoon but thinks itself too cosmopolitan to support it. Get thee to D.C., I say.

The restaurant is not the strangest aspect of the stop. In front of the business is who looks like a little person. However, he does have pointy ears. I hate to ask if he is an elf. I have been travelling with a brought-to-life Corgi steed for the elves from a fictional book after all. Elfier things have happened.

The little person says, in a high-pitched voice, "I am flipping this property." He has on a suit the color of yellow fall leaves, so I think he might be a certain kind of realtor from a certain company.

I also think he means that he is fixing up the property to resell. That is usually what flipping means in the modern context. Boy, am I wrong.

Ziggy starts to growl under his breath and then woofs. He circles me in his herding instinct and nudges me with his elongated snout away from the immediate area. We back up to where the mirrored mini-skyscraper is.

Ziggy has heard the subtle sonic beginnings of what is ensuing before I do. A rumbling starts.

Then, organized cracks around the ELFFAW Hut form. It is not from an earthquake but from some other inner workings below ground. A series of creaky gears are set into motion below us.

A rectangular pattern in the organized cracks form around the perimeter of the restaurant property. It starts to lift from the ground and flip, revealing an upside-down thatched cottage.

Then, yes, as the little person has stated, he is flipping the property. Only, it is not as we had thought.

The restaurant flips over into a hole beneath it magically and a cottage beneath it magically appears in its place.

The little person states, reading my mind, "Yes, I am an elf. Welcome to ELFFAW House."

He invites us into the thatched cottage, explaining that it was a secret hide-away for elves visiting the United States. We sit in a parlor with mostly little wooden chairs, but the elves have placed a large plush chair there for an occasional human visitor they trust. All on the walls are framed photos of elves who have had benevolent accomplishments in the United States, helping with rescuing people (sometimes with help from Corgi steeds) or feeding the starving. A wallpaper with preserved autumn birch, oak, ash, and thorn leaves within it decorates the parlor, and some small trees grew in large pots here and there.

"You have taken our steed away from one of his adventures," states the elf, looking at Ziggy and petting him.

I reply, "Well, I... just copied a version of him with magic."

"You actually did not copy him. You took a version of him from one of the Ziggy fantasy graphic novels. Look at your book," says the elf. He points with a small digit toward my bag.

I have just noticed something too. I did not have to introduce myself as O.Z. Diggs VII. Being around the elven magic must thwart the curse temporarily.

I rummage through my bag and look through it. I have not noticed before. Ziggy is no longer on the cover. Ziggy no longer appears in the panels within the book. The story has not changed. There are just blank spaces where Ziggy is supposed to be and cartoon and thought bubbles hovering above blank spaces where he once was.

I become worried, contending often with anxiety. I whine, "Will this create problems? Will the villains win in the story because of it?"

The elf chuckles and says, "Heavens no. I just wanted you to be aware that you literally brought the fictional character to life, not a copy. You must always remember that he is fictional."

"Why?" I ask.

"Never you mind that," states the elf, adjusting his autumn yellow suit, "We have foreseen some things. That is why you were brought here. You have your great-great-great-great grandfather's staff to protect you. Granted, you cannot have our magical protection like you have had now. Yes, I heard your thought about the curse and why it was not affecting you here. Anyway, Ziggy does not have a lot protection from the battle you are going to. We do not even want a fictional version of Ziggy to be harmed during the journey. He must continue in that particular printed version of his story."

From an ancient leather bag, the elf pulls out snout-guard armor and body armor. It is of the finest silver. The snout-guard for Ziggy has something resembling a prismatic crystal and diamond carved like a semi-pyramid abstract canine nose on its conical tip. The cone-shape ends in his sculpted crystal nose. The cone itself is doubly hinged and can open up for Ziggy to open his mouth widely. The body armor fully covers his body and his stubby legs. The elf instructs me to put it on him just before the battle.

I thank the elf. Ziggy licks him on the face and arms, and the elf smiles. He pulls a little pad from his orangey yellow upper suit pocket, pulls out a magic quill, and puts a little check on a To Do List he has on said pad.

I start thinking of something else now that the coming battle has been mentioned.

"My father, who I know you must be aware of, mentioned that the spirit of Mombi reincarnated. That is all he could remember. Perhaps the evil spirit of Mombi has taken over somebody else. Who is that, the one she has taken over, I mean? I know who the vile kidnapper conspirator and evil witch Mombi is."

The elf states, "The one Mombi has taken over is a collector and hoarder of items from different fantasy worlds, including Oz. She is an Irish traveler. We heard she even shoved down an elderly lady one time to get to an item she wanted at a rummage sale, and she had to be hospitalized for a while," states the elf with great sadness. Elves do not ordinarily cry, but a great pained expression is on the elf's usually soft-skinned yet sharp face. His high cheekbones seem to descend.

"How horrible!" I exclaim. "HARN! HARN!," Ziggy agrees.

I have met many Oz collectors and vendors at festivals, and none of the ones I met were like this collector; none of them had become hoarders at any price. This particular collector and hoarder must have liked to keep a low profile.

"Seeing that the human was already corrupt and greedy, the evil spirit of Mombi, upon coming here through the tunnel the Nomes dug here to evade the Great Barrier Ozma put around Oz, inhabited her. Mombi in the body of the Oz hoarder is leading the caravan of wicked witches and evil wizard in Ionia. She does not want you to go to Oz to stop what her evil comrades are up to. Mombi's headquarters is the fairgrounds, though." The elf scratches one of his pointy ears and then his diminutive head in thought.

He continues, "The possessed collector and hoarder, whose name is Catie Sheeney by the way, has squirreled away some of her collected, bought items in Chittenango, New York and is planning on going back there for them. She left behind something very important during her last visit, something in storage you will need to search for there. She won the item, fairly and squarely in an auction far away from the village, the item that you are looking for. However, you may need to... how shall I put it euphemistically ... borrow it for a while. Her other hidden items may prove useful as well. You may have to confront her and the spirit of Mombi in Chittenango. They have probably traveled there."

"Ruff! Ruff!" exclaims Ziggy.

"As she is possessed by Mombi, in addition to her own place in Syracuse, Catie Sheeney has set herself up in Mombi's headquarters in the fairgrounds in Ionia now that no fair is going on."

"The fairgrounds do not sound like much of a fortress," I say.

The elf states, with a wizened look on his face and a raised eyebrow, "You know those two metallic towers with the decorative, colorful circular rings that are around them at the front gates of the fairgrounds in Ionia?"

"Yes," I state, hazily remembering them from past story-teller visits to the town and its yearly Oz festival.

"I believe you humans have what we elves would call a lightening generator... what is it... it's something that produces electricity in a confined area..."

"A Tesla coil," I answer.

"Yes... she has made the metallic towers with the rings into two gigantic Tesla coils but with a lightening spell, and the Tesla coils do not have any grounding near them. If anyone tries to walk anywhere near the fairgrounds, ZAP! They are dead. You are going to have to teleport past those and find her headquarters in the agricultural area chicken coops there," states the elf.

"Chicken coops?" I ask.

The elf states, "Mombi through Catie Sheeney wants to force Ruggedo, the Nome King, to make more good characters in Oz into objects... just as he did with Kabumpo and Tik-Tok during the battle with your father. (I look surprised.) Oh, yes, we have all heard about your father's bravery through our magical channels.... Anyway, Mombi has played upon Catie's desire to have more and more collectibles, and Catie will be deluded into thinking those collectibles were not actually good Oz characters at one point. Anyway, Ruggedo knows this, not wanting to be forced to do anything, and is outraged. He just wants to take over the United States and gain access to any jewels here, jewels he contends were originally his Nomes' jewels just as he always stated the ones in Oz were. (Quite frankly, I always thought they were made by natural sources and were found, not made by his Nomes.) Ruggedo grew tired of doing things against Ozians years ago. He plans to come to defeat Mombi in Catie Sheeney first before enacting his own plans to take over the United States. Mombi wants to, again, force him, however, to make more Oz residents into objects. Mombi may have even more plans."

I draw my own conclusions.

"So Mombi, using Catie Sheeney, has filled up the fair's chicken coops with egg-laying chickens to have plenty of eggs to throw at the Nomes when they come."

Eggs are poison to Nomes as I knew from passed down stories, L. Frank Baum's books, and the vision I saw earlier. Eggs are symbols of fertility and of new life. Something about being old life and attached to the earth makes Nomes the opposite of these, and eggs tend to cancel them out. That is why my ancestor was using them in the battle against the Nomes back in Oz.

"Precisely right about the eggs," says the elf, reading my thoughts, "Not only are you going to have to, with the help of the Society of the Walking Cane and Ziggy, zap all those wicked witches and evil wizards of the red rebel runes to the netherworld with the goblins and evil spirits, but you're going to have to send Ruggedo and the Nomes there as well after Mombi, through Catie, does her damage to them."

I heave a heavy sigh.

"It will be okay," says the elf, "We will come help where we can if we see things have gone awry. In the meantime, there is not a moment to lose. You must continue on to Pennsylvania because there is a very important addition to your party you must find there."

"An elf?" I ask.

As if on cue, Ziggy drags out his elf plush I bought him at the antique store.

The elf in the yellow coat states, "Thank goodness that is not one our own turned into an object by Ruggedo." He thinks for a minute.

"No, the helper is not another elf but another friend of elves and many. By the way, I did not introduce myself... I had so much to tell you that I forgot. I am Legoohoos, high servant of Elf King Appoli, worshipper of the One True God, and ambassador from the elven Welsh Woods to the capitol in the United States. We were never introduced either, but I know who you are."

"I am O.Z. Diggs the Seventh. I get a little tired of having to say that under the curse but saying it to a magical creature such as yourself reminds me of my true origins as an Ozian, so I do not mind. I am thankful the curse had no affect around you. I can choose to introduce myself here."

Suddenly, I hear the sound of a toilet flushing and a sink running. Then, an elf, by portly standards for elves, comes out of a bathroom that smells like pine spray covering just a hint of scat. The chubby elf wears a small cap like they sell at truck stops with a NASCAR label on it, a pair of jeans, boots, and a T-shirt with an Appalachian folk singer on it known for using Welsh and Celtic ditties. The folk singer T-shirt is his most sophisticated garb among his attire that couples that of a cowboy with a traditional Southern redneck. He struggles over his potbelly to see to be able to scrape a bit of toilet paper stuck to the bottom of his boot off. The portly elf sighs heavily and carries a folded, yellowed manuscript copy of "The Welsh Woods Weekly."

He, who I later learn is Crudoo, exclaims to Legoohoos, "Ooo-weee... I overheard that info. dump you just gave the boy there. Well, I just had a dern info dump myself... ate three cans of elven rune soup earlier today and all those hundreds of elvish letters had to go somewhere!"

Legoohoos says, running his hands through his slick hair in frustration, "Crudoo... that is no way to talk in front of guests."

"Well, it's true, ain't it?" Crudoo stated, hefting up his jeans over his roly-poly belly, "They ought to know all they need to know just about after you got through with 'em. You dumped a load of information on them. My apologies, though, Sir, if I offended you."

I have been holding back a laugh, being quite youthful in perspective myself. I guffaw and state, "That's quite alright."

Legoohoos explains, "Crudoo is the Welsh ambassador to the Southern region of the United States. He has taken on some of the aspects of the rural Southerners to get along better with them."

The more sophisticated elf sniffs and adds, "I suspect he is half-troll."

Crudoo shoots Legoohoos a look but then takes it all in stride and chortles, slapping him on the back. Legoohoos rolls his eyes.

Crudoo knows who Ziggy and I are, so I do not do introductions with him. As he is elven, the curse is remedied around him too.

I state, "I have lived in the South all of my life. I am sure he has good relations with many traditional Southerners as a kind of elven redneck comedian."

Both elves nod. Crudoo states, "Thank ye' for the compliment!"

I state, "That reminds me. I have not been very appreciative. (I really was quite blessed in my life despite the curse on my family and could see that.) Thank you, Legoohoos."

Legoohoos states, stopping his frowning at Crudoo and returning to a more amiable expression, "Well, it is a pleasure to have met you and to have caught you up to speed on what is transpiring in Ionia and Chittenango. The situation in Ionia in growing increasingly urgent. There is not a s-elf-ond to lose (and those are quicker than human seconds). Now, I will assist your staff in transporting you quickly even after a brief rest."

Legoohoos claps three times very loudly, and Ziggy and I are zapped away with Ziggy's new armor and our other stuff to an undisclosed location in Pennsylvania before even being able to thank the elf ambassador again.

Chapter 5

The Land Bridge to Lions and Tigers and Bears... Oh My Is It High

ZIGGY AND I MAGICALLY ARRIVE AT A Clamshell Gas Station just beside a land bridge in some hills in Pennsylvania (hills to one used to Appalachia and the Smokies too). The land bridge is over a small chasm and just has enough room for two people to walk side by side with just a little room on either side for safety. Thankfully, security roped fences with chain-link are on either side of the land-bridge. We have actually ascended a hill through our magic teleportation, and I stare at the green rolling hills and the land bridge itself. On one of the hills itself is an eyesore of a billboard with some lions, tigers, and bears which reads in garish colors, "Land Bridge Zoo and Wildlife Preserve."

The Clamshell Gas Station has a large sea-green painted concrete clamshell in front of it dating back to the day when such things were used to attract people off of the highway. Ziggy sniffs at it, and I tell him, "Off !", not wanting him to hike his leg and urinate on it. I take him to a patch of thriving grass not far from a swimming pool and pet him for obeying. Oddly, a big swimming pool is located beside the Clamshell Gas Station but without a hotel in sight. It does not smell like chlorine but smells natural and slightly salty. When I return to the lot in front of the giant clamshell itself, I hear a peculiar "ding-ding-ding" and realize I am stepping on something that resembles a thin, black tentacle at my feet, a drive-over sensor to alert the attendant and/or mechanic inside.

The mechanic steps out and is carrying what appears to be a metallic trident, a device he can stick into a giant hand-pumping jack to lift vehicles entirely off the floor of his garage. The three sharp prongs of it stick upward. The mechanic has a long flowing white beard which is tied off at the bottom with blue string to keep it from dipping into the equipment he is working on. I can tell it has because his beard is pure white where his hands are soiled and pitch black.

As he approaches and leans on his trident, I say, "I am O.Z. Diggs the Seventh, and this is Ziggy."

He stares at us with wide eyes that are more aquamarine than blue and mutters, chewing on tobacco that looks more like seaweed when he opens his mouth, "I thought you were in a car. I had to come out and check." I noticed he chewed the seaweed-like tobacco more frantically when I introduced myself. On the ground not far from my feet, the attendant spits a small green glob of the tobacco or whatever it was, greener and sea-weedy than the blackish brown blobs of tobacco chewers usually spit out. The attendant keeps the majority of the green leafy chew in his mouth.

I shake my head and state that I do not have a car. I ask, "Is that Land Bridge Zoo interesting?"

Ziggy cocks his head inquisitively at the man, putting his pointy ears down.

"Well, I am more partial to Sea World myself," he says, scratching a black leathery mechanic outfit with the name "Andy" in red stitches on the lapel, and coughs, "That is, er, I think it's pretty boring. I would just keep on going if I was you."

I think of the mechanic's metallic trident – presumably used for manual jack leverage. I look at the swimming pool that is so pristine and actually uses sea salt methods. I can tell from the non-chlorine smell. Ziggy runs to it, and I yell "Off" and "Leave it" to him to keep him from drinking its salty waters. I have often presumed on my journey that the fictional Ziggy is well-trained by the elves as he was once one of their steeds. I give him some fresh water in a canteen in his bowl and pet him some behind his pointy yet velvety ears. Then, I think about why the long-bearded mechanic is so comfortable working near a gigantic clam shell sculpture and why he does not remove his gloves.

No, the mechanic is not Neptune on land, I postulate. However, he is an evil wizard, quasi-merman spy, and this gas station was set up just to spy on me. I would recognize the metallic trident magic staff of the evil wizard and merman Antoiposidein anywhere as he had it made to copy Neptune's. (I had heard this passed-on tale many times before my great grandfather and grandfather passed away and before my father's dementia.) Antoiposidein, once a handsome young merman before turning to dark magic, was known to use a spell with his trident staff to be able to walk on land but still missed the sea and converted back to mer-form periodically (hence, the swimming pool). Antoiposidein kept his webbed hands, though, so always wore gloves. Setting up shop here as a fake mechanic has probably been good for him because mechanics often wear gloves, and he will not be jeered at with his webbed hands. Rural people, no matter where they are, do not take kindly to freaks. That is universal, I have learned.

This particular merman, after the mermaids had given the blue pearl of super human strength, the pink pearl of protection, and the white pearl of wisdom to the King of Pingoree in the Nonestic Ocean not far from Oz, gave his own version of pearls to King Rinktink as vengeance against the King for helping the King of Pingoree's children once the pearls were gone. Antoiposidein magically discovered the orange pearl of weakness, the yellowish green pearl of sickness, and the tarnished or off-white pearl of foolishness in the far side of the Nonestic Ocean on the other side of Ev which is across from the Deadly Desert and Oz.

Some stated he did not discover the evil pearls but invented them from whole dark cloth, from dark magic. He gave each of these to King Rinkitink on his own island of Gilgad, and it took the jolly, portly king a lot time to recover from their dark spells. (Granted, King Rinkitink was already foolish at times, but this is beside the point.) It was said that Antoiposidein rode in on a gigantic seahorse when he visited King Rinkitink. After his misadventures with the evil merman, the king placed signs with black seahorses all over the island to warn himself of how the merman liked to travel. The now land-walking evil merman wizard will be a formidable adversary should he turn on us.

There must be some reason Antoiposidein does not want us to cross the land bridge to the Land Bridge Zoo. I tell Ziggy that we are going to cross. I quickly put his silver armor on him to protect him, telling myself to remember to take it off when we leave this battle. We put it on and off of him as needed on our journey.

We run across the land-bridge side-by-side, me holding our things carefully under my arms at my sides, until we come to some older tourists who are taking their time.

Looking behind us, we see the evil land-walking merman wizard holding his metallic trident aloft and striking it down on the land bridge, screaming, "You shall not cross!" Something about that sounds familiar yet different.

The land bridge begins to rock a little and crumble. I must stop it to disintegrate by waving my Cowardly Lion staff. I must prepare. I stop and intently focus. I focus on the lovely natural scene around us, the valley and the verdant hills. I think of Lurline, of God. The land bridge is going to quake into oblivion or at least until the bottom of the chasm if it kept this up. But I remain very calm.

Ziggy scurries past the older tourists and makes his away to the other end. A little rubble from a nearby mountain falls, just a few tiny stones fall, and it's a good thing I had put Ziggy's silver armor on him. The stones ping off of his armor. The Corgi grabs a piece of rope or vine from near the zoo and brings it back should he need to throw it to me. He looks like a robotic dog with a large wire hanging out of his mouth from this distance and with his silvery armor on. I have confidence he could have pulled me with that rope. Corgis are extremely strong pullers.

I concentrate as more rock and soil crumbles foot over foot to the deadly depths below.

Antoiposidein yells as his trident thrusted into the ground causes more and more seismic activity, "Too bad you are not on a crumbling dock on an ocean or even that there is not a river below you... I would have loved to have seen you fall and drown! However, this is not a battle of water for now but a battle of earth!"

Of course, I thought, the elementals. I am being tried as a wizard with the ancient elementals. If I survived these trials, I will become even more powerful as the ancient texts say. If I am killed by even one of the Out-World elementals, however, I will be doubly dead and not even a powerful good wizard or good witch or perhaps even an Out World mystic cleric could restore me back to earth. I do my best to breathe deeply, meditate more, and remain ultra-calm. -Deep cleansing breaths!

Suddenly, the Cowardly Lion mouth on my ancestor's oaken staff opens. It roars, and all is still.

Then, I see a small version of the malign, land-walking sea creature jumping up and down in rage as not only have I stilled the shaking land bridge, but I have moved myself to the other side through magic.

"That's alright!" he screams, "You will have to come this way again. There is a no magic barrier on the side of the mountain on the other side of the zoo! This is the only way for you to come back!"

I see Antoiposidein convert back to his other form and slither, flip and flop, and guide himself with arms back to his sea-salt swimming pool. He has a tail like a giant cod fish, which suits him, the Peter Pan insult for Captain Hook. He looks partially like one of the bass or brim I used to catch in the stream behind our cabin in Boone. The temporarily land-walking merman used so much power trying to cause the land bridge to fall and causing an earthquake to start that he reverted back to his merman form. The sea-salt swimming pool must have been a precautionary measure for many reasons. The evil, occasional merman originated as a salt water creature, after all.

On the other side of the land bridge, I pet Ziggy beneath his armor for having the rope at the ready and grab it from him to keep should we need it. "Good boy, Ziggy. Good boy," I exclaim. Ziggy wags his stubby tail which suddenly juts out from part of his silver armor.

We venture toward the zoo and a woman with salt and pepper hair in a khaki safari outfit and holding a broom runs toward us. She has been sweeping up trash as we approach and states, "Other animals are not allowed in the zoo."

I show her the aforementioned emotional support dog credential from the psychiatrist, the one that did not specify what dog it was for.

She says, "I suppose that is okay. I never saw a metallic service dog vest before, though. (She gave a wry, aware nearly toothless smile at this.) By the way, I saw you meditating out on the bridge--"

"Yes, well... oh, by the way, I am O.Z. Diggs the Seventh."

Ms. Salt and Pepper Hair in the ridiculous safari outfit does not say anything for a minute but just glares with muddy brown eyes which almost match her outfit. -Almost too perfectly.

She states, glaring, "Meditation reminds me of something some of my Wicca friends do. They get together in a circle and calmly chant for nature."

I nod.

She continues, "Wicca is a little too fuzzy bunny for me."

I state, getting very uncomfortable at her and what she must be, "I must really be going now."

She absent-mindedly sweeps the area before us with her broom, a large affair with a large handle and lots of bristles.

"You do not have to go to the ticket counter over there. I can scan you in right here if you have a card," the woman with the wiry salt and pepper hair states.

She pulls out what would look like a scanning wand to most, but I knew it was her magic wand.

"I do not have a card," I state, "I use cash only." She has a sour expression on her face and pursed dry lips.

I run to the gate and the people there are actually employees of the zoo and let me in after I pay. I have to show the credential for Ziggy again. The presumed wicked witch in the safari gear begins to follow Ziggy and me. She fools the youth working the counters with her disguise.

Ziggy, with stubby, quick paws, and I quickly make our way to a lion cage, and there HE is with his bushy mane. He is docile and friendly and does not growl at us. He, a literal shade of yellow, is not often afraid of much now but when he does have fear he knows it is controllable and healthy and that he can overcome it. He knows it is wise to have healthy fear. He cannot speak to us in the Out World but digs out a bottle marked "courage" out of some hay to prove who he is (as if I would not have known) and motions that he wants to come with us. The elf ambassador was right. We have found someone to come with us on our journey, the Cowardly Lion, of course.

The Cowardly Lion was entrapped by the witch here in this cage in this zoo so that, after being sent through the Nomes' tunnel, he could not venture to help with the situation in Ionia. As she spies on us, the wicked witch "on safari" tugs at her hair at our discovery. There are so many tourists and employees here she risks trying anything for now. She pretends to sweep with her broom again.

I take the rope Ziggy found and gave me earlier and knot it up here and there on the bars, a distance large enough that the Cowardly Lion can go through. Having gotten past the elemental of earth in a trial, my Cowardly Lion staff has increased in power and opens its mouth fast. I only have to meditate a bit. Suddenly, the rope twists and turns, twists and turns, faster and faster, imbued with greater strength from the spell. The enchanted rope has the squeezing power of 100 boa constrictors which it inflicts on the old bars. Then, CLANG!... POP! The bars bend and open, and the Cowardly Lion escapes through the hole.

He grabs me by the nape of the neck and throws me on his back while I scoop up Ziggy.

Tourists scream and run. Children gawk and are snatched up by their parents. The Cowardly Lion runs toward the land bridge. He too knows that is the only way out. He has been briefed.

He runs past the gate with us on his back. Suddenly, the safari-dressed witch rips off her safari outfit, revealing a black leather robe with red rebel rune stitching, jumps on her broomstick, takes aerial chase, and begins to shoot flame at us from her so-called cylindrical scanner (her wand), which the Cowardly Lion agilely dodges.

She has screamed, "How about a bigger fire, Scared of Crows?" She has not screamed to the Cowardly Lion and of course Scarecrow is not here so that has not been a malapropism for his name. I have often had a fear of crows or ravens, thinking them dark messengers from evil wizards and witches. The wicked witch knows this... 'evermore.

The Cowardly Lion gives a little nod to me from below to indicate that it is going to be okay. He rushes on down the land bridge, roaring and causing people to get out of the way.

The witch zooms after us on her broomstick. I try to remain very calm on the back of the lion, which is tough.

I think of a "Wicked" T-shirt I have worn underneath an unbuttoned black dress shirt at another Council meeting in one of the small North Carolina towns I cover as a reporter. It has a small picture of a witch on a broomstick and reads in green letters, "Keep Calm and Defy Gravity."

After the meeting, a woman with curly hair and a red T-shirt and a voice that could only be described as kind of hybrid Southern Belle and Winnie the Pooh, Winnie attempting Scarlett O'Hara drag stated, "I do not wish to ba'ther you. But I was offended by that witch on your shirt."

I explained that it was from "Wicked", which she had never heard of. I tried to explain what it meant, but she did not want to listen and told me that it went against her religious values. I told her I did not mean to offend her but that I would probably be wearing it again. For one thing, it fits well.

I am a relatively skinny guy but have a pot-belly from eating the sweets I like. (Many of the Diggs have skinny legs and somewhat muscular arms as aforementioned but pot bellies.) I like wearing an over-sized T-shirt over my pot-belly and then wearing a shirt over that. I only have so many Oz T-shirts to wear. Anyway, thinking of all of that took just a minute or so. I indeed focus on "Keeping Calm and Defying Gravity."

I meditate on the beauty of the mountains again and focus. The energy is being built up again.

"Here, Scared of Crows, want to play volley-ball?!" yells the witch.

She conjures up a huge fireball and volleys it in our direction with her broom mid-air, and it may have hit the Cowardly Lion and all of us (I am again thankful for Ziggy's silver elven armor). But my Cowardly Lion staff roars and opens its mouth. A huge gush of magic water is expelled from it and puts the fireball out.

It strikes the flying witch on the broomstick, and she falls.

"What a country... what a country... who would have thought that a young man (she was tempting to say Out World defunct wizard but knew that would break the spell... I could tell) like you could have destroyed my wickedness? ... I'm dropping... dropping... oooh...ooo...ooooh..." She melts as she is dropping, and her broomstick hits the land bridge. By the time it does, the wicked witch has completely melted, and her liquid remains have dripped down the land bridge. All that remains of her is her black leather robe with red stitches and black hat. Her shoes fell off into the chasm when she turned to liquid. I snatch up her red-stitched leather robe and hat and throw them into my bag.

"What a drip," I state. And though they cannot laugh in the Out World, I can tell from their upturned mouths that both Ziggy and the Cowardly Lion are amused.

Now that the Cowardly Lion staff has defeated the elemental of fire, now that I have gone through this trial, its power increases even more. My ancestors had already gained this power themselves with the staff, but it has to be regained with each new generation. Now, I will not have to meditate as much. All will come more naturally with the magic.

Speaking of water, from Antoiposidein's sea salt pool, he has been causing a gigantic tidal wave to come up toward the land bridge.

"Now you will feel the wet wrath of the magical merman!" he screams.

I feel the Cowardly Lion steel himself beneath me as I know he does not like water. Ziggy wiggles too. He cannot stand water either except to drink it.

I focus the Cowardly Lion staff toward the tidal wave coming toward us. Just a brief moment of meditation is all it takes this time.

A swirling vortex forms via my magic, a portal through the tidal wave to the next town and state, Chittenango, New York.

Antoiposidein uses his trident to give himself legs again to walk away from the sea salt pool where the tidal wave is forming. He runs on human legs to try to stop the portal. He has taken his human form.

"Fools. I have the best of both worlds! I can forget who I was and spit upon it and become something new at will! Not for love like a precious youthful mermaid... not for power like a sea witch... but for pride and for me and for the cause of evil itself!" he screams as he starts encircling his metallic trident while running and using the metallic trident as a kind of magic vaulting pole against the earth and thrusting himself into the water. His uses his metallic trident to cast a spell to keep him hovering to block the portal.

Antoiposidein jumps up sans tail into the gushing water but forgets that, as a non-merman in his human form, he can longer breathe in the aqua. His hovering spell keeps him there in the water, blocking our portal out.

The Cowardly Lion is about to jump. He has his claws non-retracted, ready to fight. Ziggy too has his silver shielded and crystal-and-diamond protected snout faced forward ready to bite. I have my Cowardly Lion staff at the ready.

It has been at least five minutes or more. The evil merman turned human suddenly realizes the sensation he is feeling is one of drowning as he tries to block the water portal. He gasps for air.

"Glu-u-u-ug" he gasps at first but cannot even make a sound after that as water fills his lungs. It is too late for him to turn into his merman form now.

The portal of water continues to swirl. I am controlling it. I am controlling the elemental of water. I am not forcing the wicked wizard merman turned human to drown, however. He has drowned through his own foolishness and carelessness.

Antoiposidein, forgetting one crucial detail about humans needing oxygen in his haste and anger to block us in a temporary human form and his pride in his own power, has drowned in his own tidal wave and sinks to the ground, dead.

I am glad the evil being is now out of the way and that the Cowardly Lion does not gut him like a fish as we jump and do not have to resort to violence in general. We pass through the swirling aqua vortex to the next state (thanks goodness the water washes us clean from sweat and grime).

What a sad waste of two Ozian creatures, though. What a sad waste that they chose to serve evil and then were vanquished through their efforts. I do not like that any people/creatures, Ozian or otherwise, have to be killed in what is becoming a kind of secret war. However, it has come to this, and, having thought my way through a lot already, take heart... and courage.

My fully-charged Cowardly Lion staff, the staff of my great-great-great-great grandfather O.Z. Diggs, with me as its latest owner, has stood trial with all the elementals of earth, fire, and water. Now, it only requires my instant thoughts to work from now on. It is better for those thoughts, though, to be kind and even in prayer and meditation. I may still falter and make mistakes along the journey. However, the Cowardly Lion staff and I have found our courage.

Chapter 6
Chittenango Falls Victim to a Witch and the R.U.S.E. Helps

WE PASSED, VIA THE PORTAL, through Chittenango Falls near the village of Chittenango, New York, birthplace of original Oz author L. Frank Baum. The falls loom tall behind us, what looks like almost 50 feet or more above to the rapids that are their source, and we are soaked to one of Ziggy's bones. The constant s-h-h-h-h sound of the falls and their hitting the rocks beside us hit our ears. I use the Cowardly Lion staff, with a mere thought now, to dry us all. I do this before the lion and canine can do their usual shaking off of moisture.

The Cowardly Lion, Ziggy, and I are at the bottom of the falls, where there is one walk-way that ascends to the main road. Above us is another walk-way with a scenic view of the waterfall below and a protective fence to keep people from falling.

Directly in front of us on a boulder on a tiny island with blue-bells is a rare Chittenango ovate amber snail which ordinarily would not be able to be seen from a distance because they are so tiny. Also, their shells are nearly translucent. However, this one, rarer still, has been made through elven magic (I suppose) to grow the size of my hand. It has a hole in the back of its spiraling shell, a shell that resembles a cochlea. Also, from its slimy protruding body, it has somehow grown two arms and hands. It has two beady eyes and a large mouth which has also been added.

The snail speaks in a proper yet squeaky way and states, "Allow me to introduce myself. The elves have given me the power of speech and limbs as well as other powers. I am the R.U.S.E. or Recording Understanding Snail of Elocution."

I interrupt and introduce myself.

"And I am Ziggy," says my Corgi quickly in a nervous yet tenor-esque barky tone.

"I am the Cowardly Lion, King of the Beasts," states the lion. I am taken aback by being able to understand both.

The R.U.S.E. states, "Greetings, Your Majesties... allow me to explain why you are able to understand each other completely now... the hole in my shell, the shell which itself is almost like a cochlea of the inner human ear, allows me to pick up any audio and amplify it to my soft interior and my own ears and enlarged brain. I open my mouth and out comes the audio translated through my shell in real time. I automatically translate the languages of all animals and humans and am an agent of the benevolent elves. I have been given the ability to speak in different languages in real time as I hear them, including animal speech."

I explain, "We are on our way to see and destroy or at least banish some wicked wizard and evil witches... maybe even some Nomes. I do not suppose you would like to come with us."

"I have been given these powers by the elves just for this journey," states the R.U.S.E., "It will be my pleasure." He continues to keep his mouth open for our words to come through his shell and then out his mouth for translation.

"Are you sure for one so small that you will be brave?" asks the Cowardly Lion, "If not, I could hunt you down a vial of courage."

"I will be," states the R.U.S.E., "I plan to ride on the back of that Corgi there. Besides, the courage potion of which you speak sounds like what people sometimes put out in tins to kill some distant relatives of mine, the slugs."

The Cowardly Lion states, "Sorry to have brought up fearful memories. I know what those are like. By the way, I would have given you a ride had you asked me, but I fear I am far too large, and you would get lost in my fur or knocked off easily."

"I will gladly give you a ride, though. Yes-yes...I am honored! Too bad I do not have my saddle, but you can hold on to my collar," exclaims Ziggy excitedly, "Yes, yes... my collar... it even has my silver tag with elven runes for anxiety and valor. In the journey I am taking in a book my master has, the elven runes for anxiety fade as I get braver and braver."

The R.U.S.E. shows that he has a necklace with a silver tag as well...only his were the elven runes for "UNDERSTANDING."

He squeaks, "Mine say, 'UNDERSTANDING' for creating greater understanding through communication-"

"MISS UNDERSTANDING!" screeches a voice behind us, "CALL ME MISS MISUNDERSTANDING!"

The short, skinny form of the hoarder Catie Sheeney rides side-saddle on the broom (something she deems proper and is able to convince her possessor to allow for), and the evil spirit of Mombi is guiding her around on her broomstick. Catie and her short, choppy red and black-streaked hair-cut, almost as short as a man's, are soaked to the broomstick, but she has not been destroyed by flying through the waterfall.

Catie states, wringing her short black-streaked yet Celtic red-mixed hair out with her fingers, "Yes... I will create a misunderstanding for you all eventually... I too am one big misunderstanding. I was misunderstood in Oz and will probably be misunderstood here too! Just as the one I possess has been misunderstood."

I state my usual introduction.

"I know who you are and know of your curse," says Catie in a voice that is shriller than her usual overly saccharine drone.

"And I know who you are and know that you are nothing more than a wicked kidnapper and the one you possess is nothing but a hoarder, Mombi!" I yell.

"She proves useful to me," screeches Mombi through Catie, stretching down a wool sweater with OZ on it in green letters, a fan sweater (one of the hundreds Catie owns), "Just as Ozma as Tip proved useful to me. Only... this one keeps me from being able be destroyed by water or anything really. If someone drops a house on her, I will just find another body!"

I state, "We will find a way... we will find a way to defeat all of you and get back to help my eternally living ancestor in Oz!"

"Also, by the way, your ancestor was little better than me... O.Z. Diggs the First was the one who brought Ozma to me and asked that I disguise her as Tip so that he could continue to rule Oz!"

Mombi tries to pat down the short-haired mess that is Catie's hair – especially messy after it got soaked.

Of course. The possession of the non-witch explains why the water of the waterfall did not affect Mombi. Mombi is now just a witch spirit in a non-witch, non-aged body. As per the other problematic issue with my ancestor, I knew of it. I just have to have confidence that my ancestor had his reasons for sending Princess Ozma to Mombi who made her incognito as the boy Tip years ago. Perhaps he knew of the impending problems with the other wicked witches of Oz. Who knows?

Suddenly, while I am temporarily in thought, Catie, under the influence of Mombi, opens a bottle with a cork and hurls out its contents in our direction. Ziggy grabs the R.U.S.E., and the Cowardly Lion shoves us all out of the way. He himself leaps out of the way quickly after doing this.

The potion from Catie's bottle just misses us. The potion mixes in with the water and goes downstream where some people are wading in and, further down, where some deer are drinking. They turn instantly to marble statues, a specialty of this particular witch or now witch spirit.

"Drat!" Mombi within Catie screams, scratching her short, now spiky gingery and ebony-blotched hair in thought, "I meant for that to hit all of you. This clumsy body... not used to magic... Anyway, it should keep you busy for a while helping all those people... I have heard your magic has ... just as your great-great-great-great grandfather's illusions did... to build." She starts to fly away toward Chittenango.

I remembered the items she has hidden away, items she legitimately paid for but one or two of them that I might need to "borrow". Legoohoos told me about them at ELFFAW Hut in Virginia. We have to beat her to them. They must be important.

I relax and focus the Cowardly Lion staff toward the marble statues and pray to Lurline. Now that I have faced the trials of the elementals, the Cowardly Lion staff's head turns to one of courage, and a beam comes out of its open mouth instantly with a magical reverberating roar. The marble statues are turned back to the forms of people and animals. They look temporarily perplexed but return to their business, unaware of what has transpired. - Lucky ones.

In the bank of the river flowing from the waterfall, while starting at the statues brought back to life, I see a toy van and an animal cracker box designed like a circus car with wheels – the type that used to be horse-drawn in the 1800s but more modern in the depiction like a trailer. Some toddler must have dropped his or her favorite toy and snack accidentally down what amounted to a ravine where we were at the bottom of Chittenango Falls.

I pocket the items, Ziggy barking that we need to go, that we do not have time to pick up litter. We do not have time to do what I wanted to do with the toy van and animal cracker box either. I just hoped we would be okay in the village with a free lion. We did not want to incite a riot of fear.

With a wave of the Cowardly Lion staff, I send us all just on the Yellow Brick sidewalk of Chittenango, an addition they made years after Oz author L. Frank Baum, who grew up there, moved away. The one in Peekskill, New York, where Baum went to military school as a lad, was supposedly old yellow clay cobble-stone-esque brick. Baum may have based the Yellow Brick Road on that.

We have beat Mombi to the village. I look at the little library with its metallic cupola. Could she, via Catie, be hiding the items she was coming back for in one of the many Oz and other very large collectible cookie jars that sit atop the shelves as a permanent collection there? Perhaps she hid them in plain sight in the witch's castle or little Munchkin house duplicated in the children's reading room there. She had purchased all of the items but wanted to hide them some distance away from her head-quarters so they could not be found there. That's how important they were.

I look toward the Tin Woodman, Scarecrow, and Cowardly Lion sign of the All Oz and Ends Museum.

I look down the street. There is a florist shop and a village crest on a brick wall. The crest has a bear on it, a scene from Oz, and the Chittenango Falls on it as well. The scene from Oz is of the Famous Four characters on their journey down the Yellow Brick Road toward the Emerald City to see the Wizard. The village crest is a large, preserved wooden circle on the brick wall.

Suddenly, we hear a horrible cackling coming from the sky, like an Oz fan duplicating Margaret Hamilton's classic performance but in the voice of Mombi trying to come through.

Ginger, black splotchy-headed Catie Sheeney swoops down toward us.

A balding, bearded gentleman with twinkling eyes peeps out of the All Oz and Ends Museum door. He looks like he wants to help but does not possess any magic power. I am not sure he can see the flying witch from his vantage point.

As Catie swoops, I calmly meditate and focus the staff toward her, and it does its usual powerful roar. It knocks her right off of her broomstick.

I command, "Send this lady back to where she most likes to go."

The magic command, via my staff, sends Catie straight to where she most likes to go... not where the spirit of Mombi most likes to go. A great gust of wind, air being controlled as fire and water had been by me before, blows her to a nearby city where she most likes to go. My control of the elementals as a wizard has increased.

Mombi's broomstick hits the Yellow Brick Road. I pick it up and carry it with me to the museum. The Cowardly Lion is very tame and introduces himself to the balding, bearded man with the twinkling eyes through the R.U.S.E. Ziggy does as well.

I present the broomstick to the man and he says, "There is something awfully familiar about this."

I introduce myself. The twinkling-eyed man does not bat an eye at my rainbow hair, top-hat, and glasses. He has seen tons of Ozian cos-plays at the local festival and even from visitors to the museum.

"And I am Ephram DeEpee. May I have your broomstick?"

I say, handing it to him, "Here... and take it with you." We both cringe a little at my redundancy.

Ephram explains that broomstick will make a nice addition to a witch display in the museum.

He must have assumed the Diggs in my name was just a coincidence as he said nothing else about it.

He does allow us to come in and says, "We do not usually allow lions in here, but for talking lions, I think we will make an exception."

Chapter 7

All Things Oz and Ends Meets Mostly Genetics Diggs

AFTER I ASK ABOUT CATIE, EPHRAM DEEPEE explains more about her, who he says he barely knows, while we look in the museum. (He has not seen her fly on the broom from his earlier vantage point.) He explains that Catie rents a studio apartment in the basement of a church converted into a bank in Syracuse and that her Oz collection fills it to the brim. He says he only knows about her because of her huge collection and that he only knows where she lives because the television stations, radio stations, and newspapers did a story on her collection.

I explain to Ephram, who because of the presence of the talking lion and Corgi tends to believe us, what has transpired with everything so far with the take-over of wicked witches and evil wizards in Ionia. He is not fully convinced that O.Z. Diggs the First is my ancestor, so the curse is still in full force.

During Ephram's and my conversations, I am amazed that words like "y'all" and other Southern words have been taken out of my speech by the R.U.S.E. I do have those, though my family is not originally from the South. We have picked them up. They have been removed, though, through the R.U.S.E. Ephram's central New York colloquialisms have been removed as well. I guess Ephram will not invite us to go eat "riggies" then. (Rigatoni with a creamy tomato and meat sauce that is a central New York invention.) He will not be able to say the term for it.

The R.U.S.E. explains to me in a squeaky voice as he holds on to Ziggy's collar with slimy elf-formed hands, "I translate everything!"

Mimicking a well-known bit of dialogue from L. Frank Baum's <u>The Marvelous Land of Oz</u> but making it my own, I state to Ephram, pointing to the translating snail, "It seems that though we are from different regions, we can understand each other now that we have a translator."

Ephram, though not getting the bit about the R.U.S.E., laughs at the reference to the Scarecrow stating this about Jack Pumpkinhead being from different Ozian regions and their silly need for a translator, though they both spoke English. Munchkin Country language is comparable to Gillikin Country language as is Winkie and Quadling and all are English unless otherwise indicated such as magic non-sense words. Perhaps only Oz fans or Ozians themselves would laugh. Some may even be tired of the joke.

We, my party and Ephram, all hunt through the museum looking for a place Catie could have hidden her legitimately purchased items in relatively plain sight. She did this so that she could come back incognito and procure them later. Hiding in plain sight was something I used to do with certain books I did not want my parents finding. If you try to hide stuff something somewhere, it usually gets found out. It becomes more suspicious.

Between the gift shop at the front of the museum and the displays which range from a black and white one on L. Frank Baum's life to Munchkin ones to ones on "The Wiz", there is an area with a yellow brick road on the floor and through a matte being shown in the distance. Ephram has just removed a black cover from it as it is brand new.

A digital camera is set up to take photographs of visitors and make a digital copy for the store and museum and an instant photo from it for the guests. Diagonally from it in the Oz gift shop for the museum are the many displays of Oz books, rubber ducks made to look like Oz characters, train sets with Oz logos, Oz plush, and countless other Oz items beyond the imagination.

Ephram points to the Yellow Brick Road display behind the camera and states, his eyes getting that twinkle they get, "You guys should get a photo so that I can convince the rest of the Oz Board I am not crazy and just keep one as a souvenir."

We, Cowardly Lion, Corgi with R.U.S.E, and I line up side-by-side on the faux Yellow Brick Road with the blue sky with fluffy white clouds in the matte background which looks like the Yellow Brick Road continues behind us.

Ephram presses the button. The digital photo is sent to his computer, but an instant photograph comes out of a white plastic box. Ephram shakes the instant photograph, which I pocket for later.

"Thank you, Mr. DeEpee."

He proceeds to take us through the exhibits. He explains that L. Frank Baum was born in Chittenango and was influenced by the rural aspects there in very early life for his Oz books but moved on to Syracuse. Nice placards of the gentleman with the handle-bar moustache and Victorian clothes and his appearances with illustrators and family line the area along with artifacts from his life.

Ephram next shows us a display of Munchkin actor costumes. The tiny clothes are vibrant green and purple. The Munchkin actors, who I had the pleasure to meet before they passed away, were often special guests of the local Oz festival, Oz-Extravaganza.

The Cowardly Lion sees all of the images and items related to his friend and himself and begins to cry a little, wiping his eyes with his tail, "Oh, I miss them all so much."

I say, "Aww... you old softy" and give him a hug. I wipe away tears myself too, though. Ziggy, being a little jealous, comes up to get petted, and I pet him, careful not to knock off the R.U.S.E. He is also concerned that I am upset as he is a character based on a support dog for an author.

Ephram is still amazed at all of this as he gives his tour. He has done a lot of performing, though, so he does not miss a beat. He has told us he is active in the theatre.

He shows us displays based on all of the actors from the M.G.M. Oz film. I notice a mannequin of the Wizard with a green coat. That is just like the one my great-great-great-great grandfather wore!

Ephram first tells us that the coat is a reproduction, that it is not an original Oz film costume. Then, he tells us that there is an apocryphal story about how the original green jacket used in the film once belonged to L. Frank Baum but ended up in a thrift store in Culver City, California. A prop man for the Wizard of Oz film found it there and used it as the costume for the Wizard. Ephram explains that the actor who played the Wizard later allegedly found a note with the initial L.F.B. on it within the pocket. I explain that not only was it L. Frank Baum's jacket but that he lent it to my ancestor during an actual visit to Oz and Baum returned it. Ephram decides to trust us further. Yet I think he thinks I am joking at times.

Ephram has decided he must do all he can to help. He knows at least from seeing and hearing the talking Cowardly Lion that something extraordinary is going on. At least, I think Ephram thinks "Cowardly" is a talking lion and not some sort of ventriloquist's parlor trick. Perhaps he sees it as an act he can invite to the village's festival. Regardless, Ephram still does not think I am a Diggs descendant. But that is fine. I did not expect him to with the strong curse going on. He seems me more as a cos-player and fan trying to help Oz. Ephram wants to help me, and that in itself is noble.

Ephram DeEpee, scratching his black beard, reveals that Catie was muttering something the one and only time he had ever seen her in the store. He said she was muttering it to herself as if to remind herself of an intentional mnemonic device, "We're off to see the Wizard... to find the coat, go see the Wizard."

"What was that again?" I asked.

Ephram repeated, "To find the coat, go see the Wizard."

Ziggy says, "The village crest depicts Dorothy, the Scarecrow, the Tin Woodman, and the Cowardly Lion going to see the Wizard!"

The Cowardly Lion adds, "I saw it myself! I looked quite handsome!" We laugh.

I explain to Ephram that we must run, thanking him again for everything. I tell him that as he can tell that magic has infiltrated reality and that we must defeat this Catie who is more than she seems and a host of others. We quickly say our good-byes.

I wave the Cowardly Lion staff and send my traveling companions to the crest leaving Ephram behind when his mouth agape. The Cowardly Lion pries opens the crest that is now before us with his claws. Ziggy stands on his hind legs to sniff what has been revealed. A hollow area in the brick is behind the crest. We find my ancestor's green velvety jacket and a small box of items such as an Oz yo-yo and an Oz cork gun. I return the crest and magick it back on with my staff. There is not a lot of time to lose. The spell I did cast on Catie to go back to the place she loved and basically stay there would not last long.

I put on my ancestor's green jacket, and it is a perfect fit. I adjust my black top hat and stuff in my rainbow-colored locks within it. Then, I adjust my green-lensed glasses. Now, I truly look the part of O.Z. Diggs, or at least AN O.Z. Diggs, as I lean on my ancestor's Cowardly Lion staff.

Next, out of my pocket, I pull out the toy van and the animal cracker box of the circus wagon with hitch I found discarded by a toddler at Chittenango Falls and place them in the road beside the Yellow Brick side-walk. Gazing from my emerald green lensed-glasses, I wave the Cowardly Lion staff over the toy van and the animal cracker box.

"This time, the Wizard has got to go to the ball instead of Cinderella, and this is his coach... well, actually first class," I exclaim and laugh with others at my pun.

Before us now is a fully drive-able van (I learned to drive years ago) with a circus wagon (made through magic to be more like a modern trailer but with the circus designs) hitched to it.

"We are going to have to quickly drive into Syracuse, a city, and there are too many people there, and many would get upset over a loose lion. People would here too in the village if there were many on the Yellow Brick sidewalks this time of day. I am afraid, Cowardly Lion, that you will have to go into this circus wagon made circus trailer," I state.

Ziggy states, through the R.U.S.E., "So this is why you picked up that litter and toy."

I nod.

Cowardly Lion says, his noble, growly baritone evoking bravery that the R.U.S.E. translates so well using an emulation of his vocal tones, "I will gladly be encaged again for the cause."

I pet his mane and pat him on the back, which he enjoys.

I exclaim, "We must hurry now on to Syracuse! We only have about 10 hours left for this spell to work and only an hour left for the one I did on Catie to work. It's midnight for the van and trailer spell to end. Why do these spells always have a time limit?!"

Chapter 8

One Messed Up Oz Fan... And You Can Take That to the Bank

IN APPROXIMATELY 30-40 MINUTES, WE PULL up in Syracuse to the church converted into bank in the magically-created van (thank goodness I maintained my driver's license and insurance) with the circus-decorated trailer hitched behind it.

The trailer is well-ventilated, and I even magically put in air conditioning in it as well as the van. So I leave the Cowardly Lion behind so as to avoid suspicion with the throngs on the sidewalks of the city. The R.U.S.E. can come with me undetected on the back of Ziggy, and if anybody asks about my canine friend coming inside, I will pull out the emotional support dog credential again. Spires from the cathedral cast gothic shadows over me as I approach its side.

The church is a quasi-cathedral of brick with many spires but has the stained-glass windows replaced with regular windows and is such a huge structure that it takes a little time to find the right door to where Catie is. Again, earlier, I had sent Catie via magic (not Mombi directly who was inside her and not in bodily form and still possessed Catie) to the place where Catie most wanted to go. Ephram, again, had informed me that this is where she lived with her collectibles according to newscasts and articles on her collection he had read.

We quickly descend through a side door, a traditional cellar door, to the basement/cellar of the church where Catie Sheeney's rented studio apartment is. When we walk in, we are not quite expecting what we find. I have heard of hoarders before, but Catie could easily be deemed "The Mega-hoarder."

Most of Catie's rooms are filled not only with shelves packed with Oz merchandise, but unopened cardboard boxes of them as well as crates filled with them. (There sat two vertical stacks of deteriorating cardboard boxes Catie had nothing to do with as my Cowardly Lion staff gave me the vision that they were bulk amounts of sacramental wine left behind from when this cathedral was actually a Catholic Church. One vertical stack was labeled, "Blessed", in a Sharpie marker scrawl. The other was labeled, "Unblessed". One of the unblessed boxes was opened and quite a few of the bottles of sacramental wine had been drunk by the priest presumably. I received the true vision that a lazy priest toward the end of the cathedral's demise as a place of worship went through the proverbial motions. He would not bless the wine in the chalice during the Lord's Supper but had blessed a stack of boxes of sacramental wine ordered in bulk. He would only do a few boxes at the time and never got around to the other stack before the church died. One stack of boxes of wine was truly blessed. Nevertheless, fully lazy in all capacities besides his handling of the wine, the priest did nothing to help the cathedral's attendance.)

Back to the boxes full of Oz collectibles and the contents of them strewn elsewhere. It's as if somebody used a cloning machine on the Famous Four Ozian characters as well as other Oz characters and put it on overdrive. Plush and action figures of them abound in armies. I have never seen so much silvery faux tin/metallic applied paint, yellow paint, blues, ginghams, and other applied colors of the Famous Four in all my life. And I have been to Oz events and exhibits throughout the country!

There are enough Oz plates, if not used for decorative purposes, to feed armies. Oz-themed furniture and nick-knacks line the ceilings. Shelves are packed to the brim with ephemera from unopened collector cards to Oz books of all kinds to premiums from food manufacturers to Playbills to props. This is the ultimate Oz collection but is the collection of a hoarder with no rhyme or reason. Most all Oz collectors or vendors I know from festivals are nothing like this, by the way. Some have large collections but not to this extreme. They have likes or dislikes and themes to their collections most of the time.

A labyrinth of stacked boxes to the ceiling allows for only a pig path-style walk-through. There are mice in abundance (and I do not mean of the type that serve the Ozian Queen of the Field Mice nor merchandise related thereof) and their coffee ground-esque excrement makes for some crunchy walking. The roaches and other bugs we accidentally step on make for some disgusting sounds as well. I tell Ziggy to leave them alone as he wants to bite and scratch at them.

Spider-webs don the ceiling beams like webbed, intricate grey mourning church hats on narrow, thin aging heads. Looking at the insects on the ground, I think of the Tin Woodman crying over stepping on ants on the Yellow Brick Road and weeping. Looking at the vast array of spider-webs, I think of unkempt wicked witches' homes and Halloween. The entire basement smells of mildew and stale water with a scent of sewage covered by sprays Catie attempts to mask them and a mild bug spray order. Some of the packages are so new that I inhale their plastic aroma just to have something else fill my nostrils. I use one almost as a mask at one point. I retch. I gag.

We make our way through the cardboard Labyrinth and finally find here there in the middle of it all, our streaky-haired Minotaur.

Catie has changed out of the wet green OZ sweater and is now wearing a Wicked Witch of the West costume with a big black conical hat which mostly covers her ginger mixed hair. Over it, she wears an open leather robe with emblems in red stitches all over it, some addition Mombi has made to Catie's wardrobe. (I have, again, noticed this black leather robe with red stitched symbols or something comparable on many who are the wicked or evil rebels of Oz, the Society of the Stitches.) Catie has a new broomstick at the ready, which Mombi has charmed and will use her magic on, for when my spell subsides.

Mombi through her, screeches, "They don't make Mombi costumes much, and she only had a few Mombi figures and not the comfortable, frumpy clothes I like to wear, so here we are!"

Ziggy begins to growl at her. The R.U.S.E. stays hidden behind his head.

I start trying to talk to Catie herself, to coax her voice forward. I think of the setting of the church as well. It has been deconsecrated and has been turned into a den of moneychangers, a bank. However, it once was a place of worship. I focus on that for a minute while I talk to Catie directly.

"Catie, you have quite the collection here," I state.

"She does not want to talk to you!" screeches Mombi through Catie's open mouth.

Ziggy barks, I shush him, and the R.U.S.E. wisely does not translate.

I do my best to be kind to Catie because the collection is amazing, though an extreme mess, "It is quite lovely, and I have never seen anything like it anywhere."

A mono-tone voice, never impressed by anything, comes out of Catie's mouth, her true voice, and states, "It is nice, isn't it?"

"Shut up, girl!" screams Mombi.

Catie says aloud but to the voice in her head, "It will be fine. Talking with this rube isn't going to change anything. You have more power than he does."

I say, being an expert of things from the Land of Oz theme-park because of my Dad, "I think I saw some nice, rare items over there in the corner that have the uniquely costumed characters of the Land of Oz theme-park on them. Land of Oz mugs, T-shirts, plates, and plush are over there the likes of which I have never seen, and my family owned and I worked in a Boone nick-knack shop!" I am just trying to coax her out more and to stall.

"You flatter me," says the mono-tone, unimpressed voice of Catie but then it changes to a voice of want, a voice of longing, "But you know I have never been able to get a yellow brick, one of the kilned yellow ones, from the theme-park. I want one or more of them so badly. I must have them for my collection. That and one of the cobble-stone ones from Peekskill."

Again, I knew all about Peekskill, New York and young L. Frank Baum being shipped off to military school there and allegedly seeing his first vision of the Yellow Brick Road via the yellow cobblestones on roads that were near the Hudson River. I had visited a yellow and green Victorian museum there which had exhibits related to L. Frank Baum's youth in Peekskill at the military school. As a story-teller, I had dressed up in a three-piece suit and put on a handle-bar moustache to become L. Frank Baum to tell those stories at an event one year. I do not get lost entirely in my thoughts, though. I have had a plan.

"Now that your voice is out, and you're being so cordial, Catie, perhaps you have been growing tired of that voice telling you what to do. Join me... join me in telling Mombi... that the power of the One who was once worshipped here, the power of God and the power of Christ drives the evil spirit of Mombi forth from you."

I cannot believe I am attempting an exorcism!

Catie begins to try to retreat, but Ziggy grabs her by her black witch costume with his teeth. "Nooooo," screams Mombi from inside Catie and begins to make Catie's body thrash, but Ziggy is strong and holds on.

"The power of God and Christ drive this evil spirit from your body. Say it with me, Catie. Say it! She will never leave you alone. You won't really be able to collect like you want. Sure... she has promised you some ill-gotten collectibles from Oz itself--"

"Shut your filthy damn Out World mouth!" screams the voice of Mombi from inside Catie, "You are no different than that little bumpkin girl Dorothy. Who are you to try to change things-"

She stops herself, though. She knows she cannot recognize me as the true heir to O.Z. Diggs or the curse will be broken.

I have thought of a couple of sub-plans in dealing with Mombi. I use the first one right now.

I pull the instant photo of all of us depicted in the Oz scene out back at museum and state, "Mombi, you are too late! There is no need to stop yourself from saying anything. There's no need to have your witches and warlocks keep guard in downtown Ionia! I have already been back to Oz!"

I show the photo to Catie, and Mombi screeches, making Catie jump up and down. Catie causes some of the nearby boxes to shake in a mini-quake. The equipment Ephram used to take out photograph was brand new, and the photograph with the digital matte image looked real. Catie nor Mombi through Catie had not seen the equipment.

Mombi's fit within Catie has given me some additional time to do the second sub-plan. Thinking of the Judaic origins of the church, the Torah or Old Testament if you will (all of the Diggs are Methodists and open to many things), I look at my Cowardly Lion staff. I pray, "I have done my best to be good and do good my whole life, God. I have been far from perfect like when my rage over-came me in Mount Airy and other times as well with my lusts. I, being connected to God's chosen, ask that with my magic ability and faith that you do just what you did with Moses and his staff, though I am undeserving."

Suddenly, the Cowardly Lion staff turns into a serpent and crawls near Catie Sheeney, near her black shoes. The spirit of Mombi screeches, "Not a snake! Not like the worms! Not like the fire-breathing 'wyrms' I left behind in that desolate, dark place before I was summoned out by the wicked!"

"The power of God weakens you and drives you out, Mombi!" I yell. I glare at her through green lenses. The snake does not bother Ziggy (thank goodness), but he manages to avoid it. I grab the snake back up, and it turns back to my Cowardly Lion staff.

I rush back to grab a bottle of the aforementioned wine pre-consecrated for the Lord's Supper. I do not have a cork-screw with me but break off the emerald green elongated top of the bottle on the concrete floor and fling the wine from the broken-off bottle toward Catie who screams and dodges it like a soldier might a grenade. The consecrated wine would have had an effect on the spirit of the wicked witch within had it made contact on she who the wicked witch spirit possessed. The watery properties of it could melt wicked witches if they had their own bodily form, and the consecrated properties of it would affect their very spirits. Their spirits could not handle it. The spirit of Mombi could not have handled it. I had read about and had seen films about the effect of holy water on vampires. The consecrated wine's effect on those who pledged loyalty to evil magic and the one who created it was comparable. The holy, blessed wine destroyed evil.

The holy, blessed wine missed possessed Catie.

Mombi screeches through Catie's mouth, "You missed Miss Understanding!" alluding to the cruel nickname she bestowed upon Catie earlier.

I reach back to fling more wine toward the body of Catie Sheeney possessed by the dark spirit.

Suddenly, though, my earlier spell over Catie making her stay there wears off, and Mombi makes Catie get on the new broomstick. The Satanic wickedness within Mombi makes her want to flee at once from this place that is getting re-consecrated, away from the sacramental wine, and away from the evoked presence of God. She uses the only corporeal form readily available to her to get the proverbial heck out of Dodge.

Catie, in a black blur with her costume, nearly knocks us over and she flies through the pig path to the cellar door on Mombi's command.

I hear the Cowardly Lion's roar outside as he probably tries to swipe at her through the safety bars on his trailer window as she passes the trailer.

We run after her.

Ziggy says, through the R.U.S.E., "Wow-wow (pronounced like bow-wow)...we almost had her."

"I tried to swipe at her on the way out," the Cowardly Lion confessed, confirming my suspicions.

The R.U.S.E. says, "I doubt Mombi will allow her to return to this refuse now – even via a spell."

I say, "Through God's, Yahweh's help, also known as Lurline in Oz, we have weakened Mombi. Her spirit has just a tenuous hold on Catie now."

Ziggy asks, "Yes-yes... but what about the wicked witches and evil warlocks in downtown Ionia? What about the Nomes?"

"We can handle 'em," says the Cowardly Lion, roaring and swiping a paw in front of him full of sharp claws.

I stated, "I truly believe we can, Cowardly Lion. If all goes according to my plan, Mombi will move the wicked witches and evil warlocks from downtown Ionia to the fairgrounds now that she thinks I have gone back to Oz after breaking the curse anyway because of the photograph. She will keep them closer to her. She may think the Nomes are defeated or may think I have retreated from them back here. Either way, she is running scared and will want the comfort of evil kin around her. Now load yourselves in, Ziggy and R.U.S.E. Cowardly Lion, stay put in the circus trailer. Brace yourselves!"

After the others, I load into the van, but there is not a lot of room in the cab section itself, so my staff juts out the window but backwards away from me with the Cowardly Lion head of it faced South when I cast the spell to transport us all further Northwest toward Ionia, Michigan.

Chapter 9

A Slight Staff Reversal Toward the South and Karl's K'onfederate K'abin

UNFORTUNATELY, I HAVE HAD MY STAFF pointed in the wrong direction out of the window and rashly have casted way too much power, and with the staff's great power, we and our van and circus themed trailer end up in South Carolina somewhere between Charleston and Columbia off of I-26 in a little town not far from Columbia in the parking lot of a small store in the air conditioned van and circus trailer. We are farther south than where I started on my quest! We are probably about 1700 miles Southeast of where we were in New York!

My Cowardly Lion Staff gives me a message that the white conical cap that my ancestor was awarded by Locasta is inside a small store in a flat-roofed, stucco building that looks like it was once a lawn mower repair shop. Hung by a pole by the doorway of the business is a Confederate flag with its blue cross of white stars of the Confederate states on a red background. A big piece of wood has been written on in childish scrawl, reading, "Karl's Konfederate Kabin" (the misspellings were all the owners and were put in for what he thought was clever alliteration). I explain to others that it's actually good that we have been sent here by the staff because Locasta's awarded cap is in there. I know the cap is in there because I can sense it through the power of the Cowardly Lion staff. What is not good is the store's theme.

I remove my top-hat and tuck every last strand of rainbow hair into my pulled-out Fedora before walking in lest I get pummeled in the store. I leave the Cowardly Lion outside lest he gets shot, according to my opinion which not all will share, I know. I see a "No Dogs Allowed" sign and do not want to explain Ziggy to the owner or clerk, so I leave him and the R.U.S.E. outside with the Lion in the air conditioning along. I take a deep breath before going in.

Karl, a Confederate re-enactor in a Confederate grey uniform with a hat with a black brim, tugs at his long, white beard when I enter the store, and a digital alert chime plays "Dixie" when I do.

I introduce myself, trying to put on a Southern brogue or drawl, "I am O.Z. Diggs the Seventh." (Westy's curse only requires an introduction like this and that I not state that I am a powerful wizard... it does not state anything about how I state it.)

"Must be one of them passed on Confederate names for y'all, your family, to keep using it. You must be from 'round Charleston with a fancy name like that. How can I help ye?" Karl asks. I happen to look stereo-typically Caucasian as I have both Irish and Austrian as well as Judaic blood in me. Otherwise, Karl would not have given me the

103

proverbial time of day. He may have even thrown me out or worse. Karl gave reenactors, many of whom do it to duplicate historical events and for no other agenda, a bad name.

I look around at the reproduction muskets and assorted Confederate flag items in the store.

I look behind the counter and see in a glass case is a white conical hat. Karl thought it was a Ku Klux Klan hat and had it labeled as such. I do not want to know how the white conical special wizard hat Locasta bestowed upon my ancestor has gotten here. I do not want to see if it has ever been used for atrocious means by atrocious people to intimidate African-Americans and Jews. I do not want to see those horrible visions from the Cowardly Lion staff. If ever the white conical hat really was used as a Ku Klux Klan hood, I know it was as much a cowardly mask as the Cowardly Lion's face used to be when he behaved as a true coward. I know my ancestor, a Celtic Jew with mixed genetic ties to good mages in Ireland and Far East Israel, did not use it as such, however. I did not feel conflicted for this reason. I just feel I need it as part of my ancestor's clothing from Oz. I did not personally use it in the wrong way in the past.

I magicked folded hundred-dollar bills in a money clip using the Cowardly Lion staff, something that I never could have done when it was not in full power as it was after I faced the trials.

Southern dialect sometimes interjects itself into my speech, having lived in Boone for so long. In this store, though, I intentionally put on the strongest Southern dialect I had ever heard around the North Carolina mountains. I gave many one syllable words two syllables, for example. Thanks goodness I have left the R.U.S.E. behind with Ziggy and the Cowardly Lion with the air conditioning running. The R.U.S.E. would have wanted to translate. My forced dialect was even stronger than Karl's, the owner's natural one.

"How mu'yech for the ha'yet?" I asked.

Karl stated, stroking his long white beard, "That there's a historical item. Behind the counter here I got other historical items too, including gen-'you-'wine Confederate muskets and ammo. You see what we're trying to sell here is history, no'yet hate."

I need the hat first. Then, I will argue with him later.

I repeat, "How mu'yech for it?"

Karl contemplates and agonizes for a minute.

He holds his hand above his pointy nose for a minute.

He truly does not want to part with the hat or really most of the items behind the counter, which to him are more like precious museum pieces.

Finally, Karl decides: "Five hun'tret dolla'!"

I plunk down the cash I magicked into my pocket earlier, and Karl takes the white conical hat out of the glass case.

Karl says, his beard flapping, "You be careful with that now, S'uh. We've got to preserve this history. They d'un took down the Confederate flag off the State House. They been talking about blasting the relief sculptures of the Confederate soldiers out of Stone Mountain, Georgia-"

"Now that I do agree with you on, not taking out that history for all to see at Stone Mountain. You see there is a wic-"

I stop myself. Not only does the curse prevent me from saying more but knowing how the person is before me stops me as well. I was about to say that my ancestor passed it along that there was a Wicked Witch Museum built in Westy's remodeled castle in Oz. I find this comparable to the depiction of the

105

generals in Stone Mountain. I cannot say this to him because of the curse. I am about to tell him that I do not agree with erasing history, not because I think that the actions of those who did malignant things in history are to be condoned but so that their awful actions can be seen for future generations. Those who do not heed the lessons of the past are truly doomed to repeat them. My ancestor (I have heard from older relatives) has tried to stop the uprising of wicked witches and evil wizards back in Oz and has tried to show what wicked witches were like in the Wicked Witch Museum. He does not erase what the wicked witches have done but displays it. I cannot say that either because of the silencing effect of Westy's dark magic. My ancestor may have been perceived as a tyrannical wizard by the wicked and did cover up some history with the hiding of Ozma (I still want this explained), but he was no Stalin. I do not want the country he originally called home, the United States, the Land of E Pluribus Unum, to become Stalin-esque and erase all history either.

However, I want the bad to be seen to educate, not the bad to be seen to state it was right. I know that Karl will not agree with me calling the Confederate generals bad, though we would both agree history needs to be preserved – just for different reasons. He condones and elevates. I criticize and put things on a real level. I tell him that I do not agree with erasing the history at Stone Mountain but say nothing to condone the Confederate Flag's placement in different places.

I thought the Confederate Flag needed to be taken down from the State House in South Carolina not only because it was used as a hate symbol but because it was used as a traitor flag to the United States. That would be like my ancestor allowing the flag of General Jinjur and her army of revolt to fly over the Emerald City instead of the flag composed of all of the colors of the countries of Oz. Confederate flags needs to be moved to museums, just as the flag of General Jinjur was in the Emerald City – at least according to passed-down stories I had heard. The Confederate flag is a museum piece. It truly is now and is displayed, according to state law, in the S.C. State Museum now.

As the Nomes had turned non-Nomes into objects and the Confederate flag represents to many people that people were virtually turned into objects as slaves, flying the Confederate flag in the United States would be like flying the flag of the Nome King away from the Nome Kingdom in Oz. It would be beyond the pale.

I know that I cannot change Karl's mind by saying a lot of this, and, again, the Oz content has been cursed out of my mouth anyway.

Karl asks, "Wasn't you about to say something?"

I smirk and back away slowly, saying in my best exaggerated Southern dialect, "I was gon'na say something, yes. Yes, S'uh!"

I remember what I said to the Councilmember many months ago when I offended her with the hat issue and later with the rainbow hair. I thought back to when one of my best friends was, indeed, gay.

We would go to Charlotte together to a gay bar that I just remember being very dark, having a lot of neon in it, and having rainbow, glowing tiles on the dance floor with booming music.

One time we even went to Charleston, South Carolina with some friends for the weekend and met some gay guys from the local culinary arts school in a Greek-themed bar with Doric columns and muscle-bound statues. Many chefs are heterosexual.

These just happened to be gay. I remember the taste of a red wine in one of their mouths coupled with a bit of orange juice and stinging strong vodka in mine. I had French kissed one of the chefs for a while. He was more of an overgrown elf; I was more of an over-grown hobbit but was a lot thinner then with a smaller paunch.

I always tended to be a homebody yet liked being around guys more than women my entire life and tried to hide it at times. I never had the intense drive to do the act that most people think gay guys do with each other. I did some fooling around with other guys and enjoyed it, but I heard a lot of people have done that. I was not completely sexually attracted to my friend, however – not at first. He was a writer as I was a storyteller, we were both creative, and he was trying to get away from a fundamentalist church mother who beat him severely for being gay. We had so much to talk about and explore. I miss him so much.

Because of our curse and because of feeling like we never fit in anywhere, my family preferred that I stay around Boone. They did not want me leaving the area much and really did not want me leaving the family business or home much at all either. My family and I shared our own secret. They thought sticking together was our only chance to survive. My gay friend and I shared our own secret as we traveled away to gay clubs.

Dad would say, "You do not need to be burning up those roads."

Mom, many years before she passed away but when I was around 19 and started going out more with my gay friend, stated in her annoying, overly-explanatory way, "It would be somewhat limiting if you continued to just hang out with him," Read "limiting" as meaning she did not approve of him being gay and my hanging out with him. At least most of the people in our Methodist Church were accepting of gay people, much better that the Southern Baptist churches some of my friends have dealt with. Anyway, these gay memories have been brought back by the thought of my rainbow hair and what I am about to do. It is going to be fabulous!

I remove my Fedora hat and bow letting my long rainbow locks fall forward over my head. My Roy G. Biv hair shines vibrantly and long like the sleeve of Joseph's coat of many colors but only in red, orange, yellow, green, blue, indigo, and violet. The promise of the rainbow shines from my head.

I state with a white lie meant to provoke while I stare at the white pointy hat in my hands in an over-excited manner, "I can't wait to make a toque blanc out of this! Wait until my friends at the culinary institute in Charleston find out!"

Karl yells, "Why you damn faggot! I outta kill you!"

The thought of this hat being turned into a chef's hat for who he perceived as gay chefs makes Karl turn crimson and purple.

Before Karl can get his shot gun and come after me, I point my Cowardly Lion staff at all of his Confederate flag merchandise and change it to American flag merchandise. I do the same with the one hanging outside as I run out to join the others. Before I go, I even change the largest Confederate flag in his store to a rainbow flag with magic. I even change the sign to "Karl's American Nook." Now, Karl really "KAN" make a difference.

The others ask me what went on in the store, and I say, "Nothing of consequence. Just a run-in with somebody too caught up in the past."

Shot gun fire ensues behind us. The others look greatly alarmed.

Nevertheless, they accept this answer as I point my Cowardly Lion staff out the van window in the right direction this time – toward Ionia, Michigan.

Chapter 10
Powder of Life Lives Matter

As I HAD OVER-SHOT WITH POWER BEFORE, I
under-compensated by shooting in less power, and
our party ends up in the van and circus trailer on an
Interstate outside of Detroit that is part of a route to
Ionia. The Interstate is the proverbial parking lot,
and eighteen wheelers and cars of every color of the
rainbow are at a stand-still on it. It is a coalition of
rainbow cars.

Blocking the Interstate is a group of Black
Lives Matter protestors who had signs in front of
themselves. They, mostly African-Americans of both
genders and all socio-economic backgrounds,
interlock their arms and keep the traffic from
flowing through. A hand-painted sign with "Black
Lives Matter" with black paint on white cardboard is
held before them. They are protesting police violence
and brutality through-out the country. The police
are there but seem afraid to do anything to
assertively yet non-violently remove the protestors.
Media vans of all varieties are in the traffic and on

the sides of the road. There are loose bricks on the side of the road where walls have been built to keep people from plummeting in their vehicles off the Interstate into trees not far off the road. The bricks are traditional red ones, not yellow brick, of course.

Suddenly, dressed in a Hawaiian shirt with emerald green mostly but red tropical flowers on it, appears my salt and pepper short-bearded wizard friend Jeremiah Strongs the Third. He has traveled here from the walking cane group in Ionia using the magic of his own staff, a birch one that is carved with a top that resembles a long piece of chalk. His staff is in honor of his favorite good witch, Locasta, who uses magic chalk and a slate to make predictions.

I roll down my window and Jeremiah Strongs say, "O.Z., we've been waiting on you! Let me see if I can introduce you in front of these people and break the spell first, though, before we teleport!"

I have to say my usual spiel. Jeremiah does not give me grief over it, though. He knows I have to say it according to the curse. He can be a jokester but not about that.

We discuss briefly his being a teacher in Indiana incognito (that's another reason he likes a long stick with chalk on the end of it) for many decades and how he has always been a part of the walking cane group that I only recently suspected was a group of wizards and witches when he contacted me via his staff. I got the message from my own staff. It was nice to put a face with the message. We had been staff-messaging each other for quite some time.

Knowing that he likes Locasta, I grab the white conical hat out of the van to show Jeremiah and bring Ziggy and the R.U.S.E. with me so that Ziggy can walk and do his business on the side of the road. The Cowardly Lion stays back in the air-conditioned trailer behind our van.

I did not expect what happened next.

"Perfect!" Jeremiah screams.

Using his chalk-topped stick, he draws a line on the highway and yells to get the Black Lives Matter protestors' attention.

Using his staff, he teleports the white conical cap to my head and shoves it down on my head. It does not cover my face but still looks quite white and pointy. This is a grave mistake. What happens next is even graver.

"This is the grand wizard!" exclaims Jeremiah at the top of his voice. He has also drawn the universal sign for daring somebody to cross, a line on the road. Jeremiah, of course, means a grand wizard from Oz, not the grand wizard of the K.K.K.

As I have to, according to the curse, I stated, "I am O.Z. Diggs the Seventh."

Angry yells ensue from the protestors, seeing my white hood-like pointy white sorcerer's hat and hearing the title of grand wizard. What a horrible title to mention and not what they thought.

"Oh, hell, no, the K.K.K. is not coming here!" screams one member.

Another screams, "Are you bringing that dog there to attack us?"

"Black lives matter! People like you don't think black lives matter, but they do! They matter as much or more than anybody else's in this country, and I will be damned if you are going to interrupt our protest with a K.K.K. rally!" screams another.

"We used to use 'dig' to describe something we like," an older African-American gentleman with peppery short hair says about my last name, "Well, we do not dig you being here. You, Diggs?" Some of the others laugh at his clever joke.

113

Then, they start getting increasingly angry.

I try to explain. Jeremiah does too, but it's too late. A rumba-rumba of the crowd ensues. Some rabble-rousers spur others to additional anger.

I want to explain that I have heard of Powder of Life creatures, very much alive Powder of Life creatures who have been treated like second class citizens in Oz. They are not given entirely the same rights as other Ozians. They are often asked to be at others beck and call and serve as guards all night because they do not require sleep. The start as inanimate objects, sometime based on other organic things, and they never ask for a spell to be put on them. However, the Powder of Life is sprinkled on them, "WEAUGH! TEAUGH! PEAUGH!" is stated, and they are brought to life against their will. Their creation and their lives are centered around the individual who created them at times. Certainly, eventually they are freed from servitude as in the case of Jack Pumpkinhead and Scraps. But Sawhorse, a sentient, talking horse made out of a wooden sawhorse by Powder of Life, was still in servitude to Princess Ozma. I know it's not exactly the same to the situation of the African-Americans who feel like second-class citizens, yet it is analogous, and I empathize. The very fact that African-Americans in the United States can be compared to how brought to life inanimate objects in Oz shows they have definitely been horribly mistreated. They have been treated as objects in the past.

I cannot explain this empathy, though. I cannot be heard over the yelling. We cannot engage in rational dialogue. Were it not for the hat perceived to be a K.K.K. one, I am sure we could have had a nice, civilized discussion. The unintended symbol I wear brings back to many bad memories for them. I snatch it off of my head and stuff it in my pocket, but it is too late.

Jeremiah explains that blocking protests like this have been going on all over the country and that even those who do not appear to be K.K.K. members sometimes cannot engage in dialogue with the protestors. He explains that even they will not be heard at times. He says that he needs to go soon and states that I should probably do the same. Other times, he says, the Black Lives Matter protestors are not listened to at all either.

"Racists!", "Bigots!", "Ignorant rednecks!" and many expletives and phrases mixed with expletives come from the crowd of protestors. I do understand their anger. It is starting to build like the proverbial pressure cooker, though.

The professor with the salt and pepper beard seems to be their leader. He says, "These white people of privilege who have been given everything (I think of my family building the store business from the ground up), who support an organization that has been known to use violence (I think of the Black Panthers), dare to come here to show that only their lives matter!"

A roar from the crowd ensues.

"Perhaps we need to show them that our lives do matter!" he screams and begins to lead others in the chant of "Black lives matter! Black lives matter! Black lives matter!"

A part of the crowd (not all, mind you) works itself into a frenzy and does not become individuals but one driving force. This smaller driving force picks up bricks from the side of the road and throw at us. This small sub-group of the larger Black Lives Matter protestors makes everything look bad for the rest with their violence. Thinking quickly, I grab two of the bricks, not to throw back, but because I think they will be useful. I think back to our earlier encounter with Catie Sheeney and decide the two bricks, though red, will be enticing for her... but not in this form.

I retreat with Ziggy to the van, and Jeremiah yells that he will meet me back in Ionia, where he is needed.

Using my Cowardly Lion staff, I direct us over to Peekskill, New York where some construction is going on near the Hudson River and where a patch of the Yellow Brick Road still remains. I have another two and maybe even three-fold plan. I need a model for a classic brick and that is the place to find it. I cannot solve the country's racial tensions in an afternoon and have to solve the problem of the ensuing battle between good and evil as a priority. This battle also truly matters.

Chapter 11
Peekskill-ed with Yellow Brick

WE END UP AT A LITTLE SHOPPING AND restaurant district near the banks of the Hudson River in Peekskill. The brownish, brackish water of the medium-sized Hudson sloshes in the distance, and a train-track runs parallel to it and ends at a small towered green and glass art deco structure that looks like it could be part of the Emerald City. A castle-like mansion home is on what I would consider to be a big hill considering my experience with mountains. Some have said L. Frank Baum saw it from the window of his quarters at the Peekskill Military Academy as a boy and turned it into Westy's castle in his imagination later. Actually, it was just coincidentally similar. Westy's castle pre-existed the castle home. In the other direction, further down the Hudson River on another hill is the colonial-esque Inn on the Hudson with its cupolas and columns nearly in view.

It is a little hard to find parking in this district because several new restaurants are being built by the same wealthy businessman among the stores, and the road has recently been worked on. One restaurant already completed is called, "Burrito Sandbar" and is a bar with a Tex-Mex and beach theme. A surfer rides a burrito in a wave near a sandbar on the sign. Luckily for me, construction gadgetry to carve brick and curbs and a vat of yellow road line paint from the highway department are all nearby. However, the parking situation itself is a pain. I park the van and allow it to magically run and send air conditioning to the Cowardly Lion's circus trailer. I ask the Cowardly Lion to stay behind again and tell him when we arrive at Ionia that I will definitely need him during the final battle. He understands.

We have actually parked on a side street behind a winery. The winery stands right in front of a patch of the old Yellow Brick Road, the road built at some point in the 1800s. It is a kind of cobblestone road of yellow bricks and only a patch of it remains. The patch of the Yellow Brick Road ends where a state road reaches it perpendicularly on one side, and on the other side, there is a row of evergreen trees ending the right-hand side of it. Because of its age, the Yellow Brick Road is a little broken-up in places but not to the point yellow bricks can be dug up. I would not want to ruin the historic integrity of the site.

I quote a movie line from a later Oz film than the classic one to Ziggy with a slight variation yet still a fairly high falsetto voice, "You don't understand, Ziggy, this WAS the Yellow Brick Road."

He cocks his head at me in a curious way and whispers to the R.U.S.E. on his back, "Are you sure you translated that right?" The R.U.S.E. nods.

I laugh after having been sad but shake my head and become sadly pensive again that this is all that is left of the historic real-life yellow brick road and examine its yellow bricks. Perhaps L. Frank Baum, the one who wrote down all the stories of Oz, had truly walked on this same road! That makes me a little happier. I take a deep, inspired breath. I examine the bricks closely. They have more of a rounded-off look that modern bricks – perhaps from erosion, yet they appear designed that way. While I stoop down, I notice tons of corks are littered on the Yellow Brick Road from bottles from the nearby winery people opened on their way to their cars at a giant parking lot near the river. People must drink wine in their cars out here.

I look at the corks and think of the Oz cork gun we acquired. I look at it briefly as I have been carrying it and the yo-yo in my pocket. Both are from the 70s, have MADE IN THE USA on them, and are from when Catie was a child. I have an idea, but something else is hitting me like 16 ounces of bricks. –Just two bricks.

Ziggy picks up a cork and chews on it. I tell him to leave it using one of his commands. He does.

I tell Ziggy I will give him a chew bone when we get back to the van. "Oh-boy-oh-boy-oh-boy" he exclaims quickly, his stubby tail wagging.

I pick it up a cork and notice that it is stained with red wine.

The snail translator from his place near Ziggy's collar states, "That is a vino rosso or red wine as is commonly translated... I can smell from here that it is from a modern time period. I am detecting hints of autumn leaves, acrid notes, and maple syrup."

We both stare at the R.U.S.E. for a few seconds.

He shrugs his elf-formed, slimy snail arms and states, "What? I was captured by a gourmet who wanted to turn me into escargot for a while and learned much in a brief time. Besides, I am a sophisticated translator. You know this."

We nod and chuckle a little. We then re-concentrate on the task at hand.

The corks stained with red wine furthers my idea. However, I still need to focus on the bricks.

One will need to look like a Peekskill brick for another plan I have. Catie Sheeney wants one to add to her collection, and this will work to our advantage.

I will need time for one of the Detroit red bricks, dipped in yellow highway paint to dry in the sun unless I use magic to dry it. Vats of yellow highway paint are not far from here as blacktop for the new restaurants needs yellow for curbs, and a newly paved road needs some for lines too.

Sometimes, one does not use wizard-craft but just craftiness. God gave me a brain, and I do my best to use it most of the time and not call upon extra powers. I quickly use some of the abandoned brick grinding gadgetry near one of the restaurant construction areas to grind one of the red bricks to have rounded-off edges. I then, putting nearby gloves on, dip the red brick into a vat of the yellow highway paint, buy a local newspaper from a newspaper box in front of Burrito Sandbar, lay it out on the grass, and put the yellow paint-dipped, rounded-off red brick in the sun to dry. The second brick, the one I hope to feign as a brick from the Yellow Brick Road from the Land of Oz theme-park, will need other methods. That will be our next stop all the way back home in North Carolina. But there is no time to go back right now. -Not and risk losing the yellow brick which needs to dry and not to risk getting covered by yellow paint dribbles. Dribbles of yellow paint would reveal my plan to whom we are trying to fool eventually.

While the yellow-painted red brick is drying in the sun (we're painting the bricks yellow... we're painting the bricks yellow... if Mombi or Catie find out, I'll be a near-dead fellow), I must gather as many corks as I can in the pointy white magic hat I am now using as a bag. Like most magic hats, it can hold an enormous amount.

Ziggy helps me pick up corks and drop them into the make-shift white bag too while the R.U.S.E. translates as we converse.

It is still the summer, so it is still hot – even in New York. The red brick painted yellow is almost dry as we continue to stoop and pick up corks. I am reminded of the fall and winter that I picked up pecans to earn money for university textbooks. Stooping and gathering can be back-breaking work.

We get closer and closer to the tall evergreen trees on the other side.

I stoop to pick up a cork near the trunk of one, and two pine-scented scratchy branches grab me.

"Who said you could take those?" the evergreen screams in a garbled voice. It stares at us with a rather wooden expression yet obvious face made of the contours of branches.

A local wicked witch in cahoots with Mombi has been given a message that I might be in New York and has brought the evergreen trees to life.

"We are the EVERMEANS!" the evergreen trees say in unison, "And we like those mementos of the cork trees!'

Before he can retreat, another has scooped up Ziggy.

Talking trees with a name based on puns, the Evermeans, make me think Mr. Baum's described world, a real truly magical place, has truly infiltrated ours.

I wiggle and grab tightly to my Cowardly Lion staff, which I have been carrying in my right hand at all times.

Ziggy bites at the evergreen or "Evermeans" branches. This does no good.

He thinks for a minute. He thinks of what is most natural for a dog to do around a tree – particularly a male dog. He is too confined to hike his leg, though.

He gets this satisfied look on his face and is very still. I hear a trickle.

The Evermean holding him drops him and in his garbled bass voice states, "Eeew...disgusting! I hate it when you dogs do that!"

I yell to Ziggy, "Run... go get Cowardly Lion."

I manage to hold my Cowardly Lion staff out toward the circus trailer to open it magically while my arms are slightly confined.

The Evermean leader holding me puts a tighter grasp on me.

He bassos and mumbles, "Oh... no... you don't... we respect the wood of a felled tree so have treated it and you gingerly... but we cannot allow you to use magic on us! We are too happy now that the witch has allowed us to communicate with those who come too near! And to think... one tourist even called us audio-animatronics... whatever that is!"

The Cowardly Lion comes bounding over to me in seconds after I have magically let him out and sent Ziggy and the R.U.S.E. after him. Ziggy is quick-pawing it not far behind the Cowardly Lion with the R.U.S.E. in tow. Already, people in the area are screaming and clutching their children close with the loose lion.

The Cowardly Lion slashes at the branches of the Evermeans with his claws, and they finally let me go.

I rush and pick up the white make-shift bag of corks and the now-dried yellow brick. We run back to the van before others can investigate, and I direct the Cowardly Lion staff to a place not far from Boone, North Carolina, a place of Appalachian clay which two unique friends I met at a revitalized Land of Oz theme-park's "Fall into Oz" event years ago use to make their art. (The Land of Oz theme-park, though closed, was remodeled and hosted several special events throughout the year.) Some of my friends near Boone have the kiln I need to make a true reproduction Land of Oz Yellow Brick Road brick.

We never stole bricks from the Land of Oz theme-park and would never have dreamt of it as family was connected to the park. But we sold reproductions of them in Nick of Time Nacks. The ones who made them for us might not charge me very much if I bring my very own brick, the second brick of many that only some of the Detroit Black Lives Matter protestors threw at us (again, not all of them were bad or violent). So I point us back in the direction of the South again, anxious to get just a few more things done before traveling on to Ionia for the big Out World and In World battle.

Chapter 12

Wallow the Yellow Brick Kiln and a "Boone" Doggle

I ONCE AGAIN HAVE TO ASK THE COWARDLY Lion and Ziggy with the R.U.S.E. to stay in the air-conditioned trailer as I venture into the pottery business of Jack and Bill, Jack and Bill's Pottery Well, not far from Blowing Rock, North Carolina. It inhabits a building made of local stone, which looks like a giant circular well. A small warehouse facility sits out back and holds their kiln. Within the circular business appear shelves upon shelves of jugs, decorative items, and even jewelry all made from local North Carolina clay.

Jack is an African-American portly man in his forties who dresses not only to the nines but to the tens as well, and Bill's a Caucasian slightly portly man in his fifties who prefers T-shirts and khakis. Jack runs the business side of things, and Bill does the art. They have both stated they are partners in the past, and it does not matter which kind to me. They could be business partners or regular gay partners. Why should it matter?

I do remember when I was in middle school that it did matter to me in the sense that I was closeted. Plenty of straight guys like fantasy and science fiction, but my liking creative things like writing which I mostly read aloud dramatically for fun was suspect in the rustic area just outside of Boone where I grew up. The country boys saw that as too soft for boys to enjoy. They also thought I was snooty when I always had, via the curse, to introduce myself via my title.

Yes, my cabin is technically in Boone but is in more of a rural area. The school I attended was further out from Boone. Anyway, I used to adamantly deny that I was gay when people would pick fights with me because of it. I would get into fist fights to defend what I thought was my honor at the time. I never fought in elementary school and stopped getting into fights in high school. However, my uncontrolled temper really got the better of me in middle school. I am not averse to fighting now in these battles but realize how very angry I get and how intense my rage is. I had succumbed to it several times already on this great journey and had mostly mastered it. Anyway, I was still closeted in high school but kept my head down about it. I was cornered in the gym locker room many times and had to fight my way against crowds like a bull or bear fights a pack of wild wolves because of their accusations of my being gay. Group bullying was a way of life then and was seldom if ever talked about or stopped in small Southern towns or suburbs. Anyway, it should not matter if Jack and Bill are gay partners and/or business partners. They do not seem closeted like I was in the past. It is just hard to tell. My gay-dar is broken. My Cowardly Lion staff does not come with gay-dar or a spell to detect gayness. I do the best I can.

Gay or not, Jack remembers me from the seasonal "Fall into Oz" events where Bill and he were both vendors while I was a performing story-teller, and I tell him about my urgent problem.

Before I did, I state, "I am O.Z. Diggs-"

Jack, the African-American gentle-man, interrupts in a proper, almost British voice which floors some white racists, "Yes, I remember. What can we do for you?" I guess that counts toward fulfilling the curse or perhaps it has indeed weakened.

I explain what I need and the urgency of the situation. Well, I state it is for a gift needed for today. So I have a bit of a sin of omission. It's a faux gift. So sue me.

Jack, staring at me with brown eyes, says they could have the regular red brick kilned with a yellow glaze, just like the classic yellow bricks at the Land of Oz theme-park, ready within the hour. He rushes this in front of some other projects, but it will not take up a lot of space in the giant kiln anyway. I will have my classic faux yellow brick seemingly from the 1900s but will also have the faux 70s Oz theme-park-style kilned and glazed yellow brick. Both will indeed prove useful, I just know it. Catie Sheeney's an avid collector and wants these bricks more than just about anything. A collector who also happens to be a hoarder will stop at nothing to get his or her next find. Catie herself knocked down an elderly lady to get to her latest find once. Legoloos had told me.

Seeing that he has a new job to do, Bill grunts that he better go get busy, adjusting a clay-stained T-shirt which reads, "Artist at Work", and Jack shows us around the pottery showroom.

Bill says, as he quickly walks off to the kiln facility, "Looks like I've got another miracle to perform!"

In the meantime, his business (or otherwise) partner Jack shows me some witches and Jack O'Lanterns he had made for Halloween. The pottery Jack O'Lanterns could hold candles within them and had holes for the eyes, nose, and mouth just like regular pumpkins.

Jack pulls a white silk handkerchief out of his lapel pocket and wipes his slightly balding light brown head with it as he shows us around. We seem to be going in circles but are covering the circumference of the entire store because we are in a gigantic building made to look like a circular well. I notice Jack particularly wipes his head while showing us the face jugs within the business. He becomes more excited when discussing them.

Jack says, "You already know the history of the face jugs, O.Z. You can see we have a plethora of modern ones here."

Face jugs were most often made by African-American slaves in the South. The face jugs often had relatively grotesque (the style, not ugly) appearances and had exaggerated features. Sometimes, the jugs would not have handles. Sometimes, the "ears" of the head depicted on the jug would be handles. Each face jug had its own distinct character and individuality. At least, that has been how Jack tells me they should be made.

He even states at one point that some people thought that people's souls themselves could travel into such vessels. I listen to this with great interest. After all, we have a spirit we need to get out of a body and contain somehow. If a face-jug could somehow contain it, we might better be able to get the soul of Mombi out of this world.

We almost move from that area of Jack and Bill's Pottery Well when I notice something. A face jug with the face of a hag like Mombi sits there on its own side table. The jug is the size of Catie Sheeney's head but had the long, seemingly greasy yet clay locks of a hag. The face has a permanent scowl, and the nose on it has a few clay warts. They have, of course, colored it green with pigment and a bumpy glaze to evoke warts in the kiln.

Jack states, "That's something we just did for Halloween coming up in a few months... like we did the other holiday items."

I ask to buy it from him.

He states it will be about $300. I give him some of the money I had magicked earlier.

By that time, the yellow brick is ready, and I want to go check on Dad in Boone. I thank Jack and Bill and state I will see them at the next Fall into Oz, and Ziggy, the R.U.S.E., the Cowardly Lion, who waited in the a-c, and I get on the road with our yellow brick and the face jug.

Dad is fine and has long arrived by the time we have come in to my place at Boone to check on him... and I do mean all came in. My cabin is off the beaten path in the valley by that stream I mentioned earlier near the water-mill, so no one would be alarmed at a lion coming in with us. No one could see him there through the patches of woods except for us. I have hoped Dad will remember who the Cowardly Lion was with his recovery from the dementia spell from Ruggedo. Thankfully, he does. After our usual cursed familial introductions are over, Dad says he is over-joyed that I had found all of my ancestor's clothing he left behind.

I pull a defrosted steak of Dad's out for the Cowardly Lion and tell him that it will have to do for him to survive because I do not think he would eat tofu and we have no faux meat that would match Oz's here. I also feed Ziggy some canned chicken and put out some lettuce leaves for the R.U.S.E. All are too interested in eating to talk at first.

I nibble on a peanut butter and jelly sandwich I made and bring one to Dad as well.

I tell Dad all that had transpired so far, and he remembers better the part about the spirit of Mombi and who she had possessed now. He could not tell me any more details other than that she was around when I had found him a few days back after his years being lost in West Virginia. His memory has recovered in many other ways, though.

I show him the face jug which I had brought in. I had left everything else in the van.

Dad states, "A Gollum."

"You mean that little hobbit turned nasty in The Lord of the Rings?" I ask.

Ending in more of a Corgi ra-roo, Ziggy jokes, as he stares at the discarded gold-colored ring-top of the canned chicken, "My precioooooooooooooous!"

The R.U.S.E. states, "At least that's not a tin of escargot. Slug-sies instead of second-sies... after arugula appetizers instead of second breakfast... I could see non-hobbits like that gourmet I was around eating all kind of things that make me shudder." He has been opening his mouth after swallowing bits of lettuce so that his magic cochlea can continue to translate.

"No," Dad says, laughing, and his own cleverness returning more and more with even an occasional impression, "No decrepit, soul-seared hobbits like Gollum and no NASTIES appetizers! Gollum is a name for a clay creature brought to life by the Eastern European Jews by putting the true name of God on it. The true name of God brings the clay figure to life just as Adam was brought to life with Yahweh's breath."

The Cowardly Lion has finished his steak and has been licking blood from his chops when he states, "Kind of like how Jack Pumpkinhead and the others were brought to life with Powder of Life in Oz."

The R.U.S.E., still hanging on to Ziggy's collar, has been able to translate for the animals through his magical cochlea shell and with an open mouth after finishing his lettuce.

I state, "But this isn't a Gollum."

Dad says, "But it could be. Hear me out." Dad is indeed getting his mind back. The R.U.S.E. jokes, "I always 'hear' people and creatures out." We roll our eyes but chuckle.

Dad narrates, stroking his long white beard in thought, "We, long, long before my great-great-great granddad went to Oz, were descended from Middle Eastern Jews who traveled to Europe and became clockmakers and watchmakers and who eventually married Austrians and then blended into Ireland because quite a few Celts derived from Austria itself at some point. Our Jewish finally also married into the Scots-Irish. Orthodox Jews would be dismayed."

"Some purebred Pembroke Welsh Corgis do not want to marry Cardigan Corgis and certainly not non-Corgis. Not me, though, I'm not a snob," states Ziggy matter-of-factly.

"Clockmakers, eh? That explains why you thought that elephant and Tik-Tok clock Ruggedo made out of some of our Ozian friends was one of our heirlooms," I remind Dad. Just about a week ago, he had made dementia-based mistakes about the clock's origin.

Those mistakes coupled with many others could be heart-breaking. I wish there were some way to un-magick that part of our lives away, that part where Dad had lost his memory. There were times when he would not remember even the closest of immediate family members, and he would just get that glassy stare. I did my best to wipe that from my mind, a forgetting of the forgetting. It was time to do my best to let go and try to move forward.

He remembers and says, "Yes, I had it all wrong. I remember now that Nome King Ruggedo wants to turn Oz residents into objects. Really, he is doing that to appease Catie Sheeney, influenced by the spirit of Mombi."

"ROAR! We will defeat the Nome King and all of his ilk!" yells the Cowardly Lion after finishing his steak. He seems invigorated. His roar and screamed baritone promise made us not only leap but do virtual jumping jacks.

"We will. We will, Cowardly, my friend...stay calm for now... Still, I do not understand what this family history has to do with the Gollum," I state. I do not intend any disrespect. I love him dearly. Dad could perform well from a script as the Wizard at the Land of Oz theme-park. He can follow a set of instructions of most any kind to the letter in his prime and especially now that he has his mind back. He just cannot tell a story to save his life. He never has been able to, even with his full faculties. Things are all out of order.

"Be patient, son. Someone in our family actually made a clockwork Gollum one time, a faux Gollum, for a wealthy patron. This messing around with clockwork and theatrics was passed down to our showman grandfather who ended up in Oz. Perhaps you could fake bringing this hag jug head to life," replied Dad.

The Cowardly Lion states, settling down for a brief nap after his meal, "I can definitely tell you both descend from O.Z. Diggs himself with this plan!"

"Yes... I could fake bringing it to life with Powder of Life. I will just cast an illusion spell on the jug head of the witch and sprinkle any white powder but salt on it," I add. I state "not salt" because I do not want to fend off the evil spirit of Mombi with salt. I want her to enter the vessel.

I explain to Dad that the African slaves who did jug head pottery sometimes thought that spirits could enter the jug.

I ask, "Will we really need to appear to bring the jug to life then?"

"Mombi is a tricky one," Dad spits the words out (he had been thinking of all of this after he had started remembering about the spirit of Mombi and everything), "She was a master of Powder of Life usage and would not be fooled by any fakery related to it. And it would be reeeaaaal hard to capture her spirit in a jug. However, if she were to go willingly--"

"I see what you mean. We could make the hag vessel appear to be a talking face with other magic. But would she just go to a talking face jug?"

Dad ponders aloud, tugging at his beard in thought, "No...you're going to have to have somebody look like a person with the head-jug as a head. Make a Headless Horseman-style costume like they do at theme-parks for Halloween events sometime. Make a flat piece and put it at the top to put a fake head on where the head is missing. Better yet... just find one premade." He was used to such adaptations in his own work at the theme park.

I tell Dad that I will probably have Jeremiah Strongs III, one of my fellow wizards there do it, wearing the costume, as I would be very busy implementing other parts of my plan. I let him know that I think it will work, that the spirit of Mombi will try to inhabit the very powerful looking, ancient tall hag dressed in Headless Horseman black once we run her out of Cattie Sheeney. Mombi will have to do so through the mind, through the head and will end up in a clay vessel face jug that from a distance she has only thought is a head. Having the face talk like a faux Gollum will fool her if she thinks it is on a real body. Also, the face jugs were said by slaves in the past to capture souls, so the jug will capture Mombi's transferred soul for a while. Then, the good wizards, benevolent witches, and I will find a place to send Mombi's capture soul in the face jug. It will be like sending the evil genii in the lamp back to a hideaway.

I shiver as I have a feeling I know what "hideaway" we are going to send her to. I tell Dad I am grateful he is okay and made it to my cabin and that I will use his part of the plan but had to run. I give him a gigantic hug good-bye.

My brave father wants to come help, but I explain that as he was weakened mentally after Ruggedo's attack years ago and was still slowly recovering that he better stay behind. He understands and says that he will meditate and pray and send what magic he can to help.

Before I had left, the time had come to talk of many things, of reproducing Catie Sheeney's cork gun like I do money with magic, of doing the same with the Oz yo-yo she left, of yellow brick gifts, of a faux witch, of corks, and, finally, of those bottles of blessed wine left behind in the basement of the church at Syracuse. These have all been parts of my plan, and the wine in Syracuse is where we were headed next. –The wine that was with the whiner!

Chapter 13
Robbing from the Rich

As NIGHTFALL APPROACHES IN SYRACUSE, I start loading boxes of the blessed wine into the van and partially in the Cowardly Lion's trailer. I get brown dust on my arms and face from the disintegrating cardboard in places and the filthy-ness of the basement. I figure it will take all of the boxes, though, and have to keep going back to load more. I am completely filthy with brown dust from head to toe and need a bath.

Once we arrive at the fairgrounds in Ionia or soon before, I plan to get a shower using my magic with the elemental of water. Then, I plan to replicate the cork gun of Catie Sheeney with my Cowardly Lion staff just as I did money in the past and dip the many corks from the Peekskill winery in the blessed wine and load them in the cork guns, recruiting Ionian citizens as Ozian deputies. Any wicked witch or wizard shot with one will be vanquished and any wicked spirits inhabiting other mostly non-wicked people will be too! I have chosen the blessed wine because of its effect on evil magic users and not water, which sometimes has been known to kill witches. The reason is that water does not tend to get completely absorbed in a cork the way that wine does. Water evaporates!

I was afraid it would dry by the time each cork hits the witches and wizards. I had plenty of time to ponder that during our time in Peekskill. I had observed the consecrated/blessed and its effect on the spirit of Mombi within Catie Sheeney. Now, I have that holy wine loaded into the trailer behind the van. I have managed to extend the spell on it and the van itself another day, by the way. —Now for part of the cork and other parts of my plan.

Anyway, Catie's cork gun is a really old-fashioned kind without a string to retain the cork for safety. It was decorated in an emerald green and had an O and a Z on it and was meant to duplicate the one from the Soldier with the Green Whiskers, the musket with the flowers sticking out of its muzzle.

Catie's yo-yo has an O on one side and a Z on the other and was an emerald green as well. I plan to magically combine one with two eggs, one on each hemisphere of the yoyo and egg-yo if you will and have them be used as weapons against the Nomes. Catie, as I recall, had already done most of the work for me on this as she had, according to the elf ambassador I met earlier in my adventure, loaded down the chicken coops at the fair-grounds with egg-laying chickens as well as many additional eggs from outside the fairgrounds in anticipation of the Nomes. I knew how to combine these eggs with yo-yos via the combination spell I learned from my father. It was good for mixing him cocktails he sometimes wanted with the local remedy – an occasional vice he subscribed to.

I also remembered from some Asian stories I told at some festivals that yo-yos were originally invented out East. They could be used as distraction weapons for those into martial arts, much like fireworks were. I used to read tons of books on various subjects from the library before reading more storytelling and fiction books in my older youth and adulthood. I plan to use this information to my advantage.

I know the benevolent wizards and witches of the Society of the Walking Cane with their staffs hidden as walking canes will be able to produce many spells to help. However, the throngs of Nomes and wicked witches and evil wizards might require other magic battle items. I have done my best to use my noggin along and along to prepare for the final battle.

Before loading some final wine boxes, I decide I better attempt to replicate at least one pop gun and at least one yo-yo before going on to Ionia. I will have to practice combining a yo-yo with two eggs before duplicating it and making others when I arrive in Ionia.

I hover the Cowardly Lion Staff, with its empowered courageous face set to roaring through the power I have earned, over Catie Sheeney's objects to duplicate them. The Cowardly Lion staff does this.

The staff, thinking I will also want to know what transpired then, flashes me back to when the objects' owner was younger. Suddenly, a red-haired and pig-tailed young Catie Sheeney is shown with her father at a combined bus and railroad terminal in New York City. She, in a gingham dress she picked out because she is an Oz fan, is sitting with him on a bench, and her feet do not reach the floor. Her father is dressed in a khaki London fog and dress clothes.

He, a morbidly obese Celtic man with bushy hair and eyebrows, has a gigantic suitcase with him nearly the size of a steamer-trunk. Leaned against the steamer trunk is a bamboo cane.

"The Wiz" is popular during the time this scene the Cowardly Lion staff is showing me. Even some cart vendors and gift shop vendors are selling Oz items, which is where Catie's father bought her Oz pop gun and yo-yo at the last minute as going-away presents.

This is what the Cowardly Lion staff showed me happened then.

The portly Irishman with the flowing locks, Catie's father, played her an Irish ditty on a fiddle he produced from a case that is inside his steamer trunk, careful to put the bamboo cane gingerly beside it again. Catie stretched downward to tap her feet on the floor some to the ditty and makes her Oz pop-gun and yo-yo dance in her left and right hands to the tune. Her father played Catie her favorite tune for what seemed like 30 minutes. Then, he stopped and became very grave.

"Catie, I have to go away for a long time now," he said.

Catie was old enough to know what this meant. She hugged him but then clutched very tightly to the Oz gifts he had bought her.

She whispered, "No."

"Catie, now, be reasonable. Be a good girl."

Her large father walked away on his bamboo cane, dragging the steamer trunk with the fiddle case, clothing, and other items within it behind him.

Her mom came from the corner of the station to pick her up.

"No!" Catie screamed, getting louder. (I start to see partially how Catie became the person she became.)

People watched as Catie screamed, clutching her Oz toys very tightly as her mother took her away, and her father left, never to be seen or heard from again, "NOOOOOOOOOOO! NOOOOOOOOOOO!"

....NO!" screams a policeman, breaking my concentration, "No! Put that box down and put your hands up."

He has seen me looking like a person of color with the brown stains on my skin in the dark. I think he assumes I am stealing as a person of color. Well, I am technically stealing, but it is for a good cause, and it's something that is no longer being used.

I finish loading the last box before he starts drawing a weapon.

I then draw out the only weapon I know. Only, I do not shoot the policeman. I do not answer violence with violence.

Instead, using magic, with my van, circus trailer, and friends, I leave the situation with the policeman with the drawn gun and head on to Ionia with my newly acquired boxes of holy blessed sacramental wine as evil spirit deterrent, leaving a very annoyed yet very perplexed cop behind.

Chapter 14
The Chicken Trailer of Oz

I DO NOT HAVE MUCH TIME TO PONDER ABOUT how I was treated by that particular cop when I appeared like I was a person of color. However, I will say that I empathize even further with the plight of most of the Black Lives Matter protestors in Detroit. I do not condone the actions of those Black Lives Matter protestors who threw bricks, though. Those potentially fatal actions are no better than police violence. Cops have been hospitalized in I.C.U. after being hit by bricks. Cops have also been shot in cold blood. With the proverbial eyes for eyes, we're all blind.

With my Cowardly Lion staff set to roar, I produce water as if with a showerhead and wash what I was judged for, the faux color of my skin, off. The majority African-American Black Lives Matter protestors cannot, of course, wash away the color of their skin and have assumptions made for it. What I also do not want to have the appearance of is one of the old minstrel shows. I do not want to be perceived

139

as racist again nor do I want to be perceived, albeit wrongly, as a thief of color.

Though I cannot fully understand it as I am a person of Celtic Judaic origin, I have felt the African-Americans' anger and pain, albeit briefly. I cannot imagine living with it for a lifetime yet do not feel personally guilty about white people's mistreatment of black people in history. I do not feel guilty because my ancestors came over during the Great Famine from Ireland and were treated terribly for being Irish and Jewish and never owned slaves. I do not have "white guilt."

Plus, being Ozian, the original O.Z. Diggs had passed down a love for all people regardless of color or even form through my entire family. We even originated from a fantasy world without the kind of slavery as seen in the United States and other countries in the Out World. Our business in the Out World, Nick of Time Nacks, always sold goods to all races and hired all races through all time – sometimes catching flack for it from local rednecks. We never did what some families did, not invite black children to their white kids' birthday parties. (Yes, this even happened in the 70s and 80s in the South. I have heard of it happening in largely segregated parts of Northern cities as well.) I do not condone racism against African-Americans nor do I condone the mistreatment of African-Americans by police. What I also do not condone is the violent actions of some of the protestors. I do not condone unjustified violence from police officers. Violence begets violence.

Unfortunately, I am going to have to use violence in addition to magic to rid Ionia of wicked witches and evil warlocks, and I must continue my quest with my friends and pontificate on racism more later. I am really going to have to control my rage in the upcoming battles ahead and not against other races but wicked witches and evil wizards of all ethnicities. I park the circus trailer and van in a large space reserved in the blocked-off downtown of Ionia for various retro-RV's and retro-travel trailers. Some of the travelers are good witches and wizards. Others are evil. Still others are non-magic users.

The Society of the Walking Cane members have mostly stayed at a local hotel. However, there are a few with vintage cars and vintage silvery trailers (perhaps with real silver coating to ward off evil) who have parked and stayed downtown. They are in their own encampment well away from the evil ones.

Trailers and recreational vehicles of all shapes from rotund to squarish and all colors from green to violet among others line the blocked-off Main Street along with vendor tents that sit outside a historic early 1920s art deco cinema and houses and two and three-story shops that mostly have Victorian architecture. I figure the hot colored vintage trailers are owned by the evil ones. Vendors tables selling Oz merchandise and crafts line the sidewalks of the downtown for people to shop from during the Oz festival. Guest Oz authors, storytellers, and celebrities are placed under the marquee at the historic cinema or in part of the lobby. The lobby of the cinema and the cinema itself are decorated in the most amazing blend of art deco and Native American décor. Just outside in the downtown, the wicked witches and evil warlocks have abandoned their trailers and recreational vehicles here to teleport themselves to the fairgrounds and help Catie Sheeney possessed by Mombi.

Jeremiah Strongs III has found me and is approaching with his long staff with the chalk-like top and his silvery locks blowing in the wind.

Jeremiah states, "I see you made it unscathed, O.Z."

I have left the others in the air conditioning. I introduce myself as per the remnant of Westy's curse, but he stops me. I then tell him about the others in the van and circus trailer.

Jeremiah yells to Cowardly, "Cowardly Lion, so nice to have you here. You will be a grand asset! Ziggy and R.U.S.E., it's good to have you here too. We were not properly introduced during that debacle in Detroit." The others give him cordial greetings. He had magically used telepathy to learn about the R.U.S.E., it seems. I tried to shush Jeremiah a little because I did not want everybody knowing about "Cowardly" yet.

I explain to Jeremiah the plan about the face jug and the need for a Headless Horseman costume and that he will have to wear it.

"That sounds like a grand plan, O.Z.," he states and, ever being the teacher, states, "Quite academic too, man!" He tugs at his white beard deep in thought, thinking of all of the possibilities.

I also explain to Jeremiah what I have gathered as weapons and how they will be used with blessed sacramental wine alongside the enticement of the collectible yellow bricks for the possessed Catie Sheeney. I tell him the Society of the Walking Cane will be a wonderful magical army but that the group will need help.

"While you seek out a Headless Horseman costume," I state, "I will be seeking non-magic-user recruits downtown here. Meet me back inside the Ionia Fair Grounds. Remember to teleport directly inside the fairgrounds. If you go near the gates, the giant Tesla coils will get you...although I do hope to have those down by the time you get back."

"No worries there, man", says Jeremiah, "One of our members made the mistake of taking a practice walk by there. It was all she could do to keep from being zapped by using her walking cane staff to shoot the electricity back. She was almost toasted!"

Jeremiah says the Society of the Walking Cane members, for their main walk incognito as a senior citizen group that travels to different places to do hikes, had been slowly walking toward downtown Ionia where the wicked witches and evil wizards had gathered in some of the travel trailers and rec. vehicles. He states after I told him in Detroit that Mombi, through Catie Sheeney, was moving all the evil witches and wizards from downtown to where she was in the fairground that they had started their relatively slow walk back. He states they should arrive there any minute as they were taking a scenic back route.

I tell him I appreciate the up-date but that we better rush.

"It's late June," I state, "Other than a theatrical troupe putting on an unseasonably early production of 'The Legend of Sleepy Hollow', I do not know how 'in Oz' you are going to find that Headless Horseman costume, though it was my father's idea to couple with the hag face jug and a good one. I guess you could always make one with magic."

"You forget I am wily, albeit a little more positive than most who are," Jeremiah blurts through chuckles as his bushy eyebrows lifted and he got a wide-eyed, almost crazed look, "I have gone to Salem, Massachusetts to see how the Out Word-ians treated witches of all types. Let's just say it was not very pretty at all. Anyway, not far from there, around Boston, I discovered that there are Halloween outlets opened nearly year-round or at least wicked early in the year as they would say. There's enough of a Celtic population around Massachusetts that Halloween is a REALLY BIG DEAL." He states he will have no problems getting the costume.

With this, he gives his goodbyes and promises to meet us within the fairgrounds within an hour or so via teleportation or some other method back to Michigan after going to Massachusetts the same way. Making sure no one sees him as he is behind a yellowy trailer, he draws a portal mid-air with chalk, walks through it, and disappears.

The yellowy trailer, though, once Jeremiah has used magic around it and has disappeared, suddenly ascends with chicken legs. I kid you not – real chicken legs. As one well-versed in fairy tale lore and telling fairy tale lore, this does not really surprise me. Why, it is just a modern version of the hut of Russian witch, Baba Yaga. Her hut in the woods was also on chicken legs and could be moved around.

Beneath the trailer, I notice some eggs laid from the chicken portion of it, a large chicken posterior at the aft end of the yellow trailer that keeps the legs connected to it. I collect these eggs to put in the van, the trailer not able to make any noise. Its owner of the chicken-legged yellow trailer, wicked witch Baba Yaga, has gone with the others to join Mombi.

I remove any magical protection spells on the trailer with my Cowardly Lion staff with its roaring expression. I then commandeer it for our efforts against the Nomes who will eventually be coming after Catie Sheeney and Mombi. Not only will we have to deal with the wicked magic users, but we will have to deal with Nomes gone wrong, particularly Ruggedo who has returned to his old way thanks to the evil magic users' meddling.

We can always use extra eggs to supplement the ones of the many chickens Mombi through Catie Sheeney has gathered in the agricultural center's poultry gigantic barn-filled section of the fair. And we can use the trailer on chicken legs as a kind of walking military vehicle of sorts.

What we will also need is assistance from non-magic users.

Seeing plenty of bills and other paper littered here and there, I turn my Cowardly Lion staff into a kind of wave-able copy machine. Its only copying noise is a roar it makes with each duplication. On to the bills and other paper litter, I copy the message with plenty of graphics of wicked witches and evil wizards being obliterated, "Come to the Ionia Fairgrounds during the Wizard of Oz Fest Ionia. Come for Baum and Baxley Fair entertainment! Marvel at the brand new robotic figure paint-ball-gun craze rocking the nation! Shoot figures of wicked witches and evil wizards with specially-designed paint-ball guns. Prizes for the most wicked witch and evil wizard figures hit! –Trained, tame lion on premises! Meet at the fairground at 3 p.m. All of the power issues and electrical problems will be solved by then!"

I realize this will mean I will have to get rid of the Tesla coils at the ringed-columned gates by then. The local newspaper, I had heard, has been calling it a huge electrical failure and the local power company has been investigating. A few people were killed who walked near the fair very recently through electrocution. It kept people from going there. Jeremiah Strongs III stated even his fellow members in "The Society" were alarmed by it.

I also realize that technically the duplicated cork guns are not paintball guns but with the wine-dipped corks and no strings attached to air guns made more powerful through magic, the effect will be the same. I will juice them up too. I will make it look like with extra boosts of air magically infused in each one that they are mini-paint guns. I know many enthusiastic youth and big kid adults will jump at the chance for this.

The Cowardly Lion will be able to roam free and help in certain areas at the fair-grounds now that I have advertised that he is a trained, tame lion and part of the mini-carnival.

I distribute the fliers all up and down downtown. I even have Ziggy hold some in his mouth and carry to people, which they think is very cute. I ask the R.U.S.E. not to translate for him, though, because I do not want to alarm the Out-World folks with a talking Corgi. Cowardly Lion has to stay behind in the a.c. again lest we cause a gigantic scene and unintentionally foil our own plans.

As I am distributing the fliers, the coordinator of the festival, Laura, a middle-aged woman who appears to be at least a decade-or-more younger, rushes over to me with one of them.

I introduce myself yet again for the umpteenth time.

She states, laughing at first, in her Midwestern dialect, "Of course I know who you are. It's so good that you were able to come as a story-teller. About this flier, though, this was not authorized. We have not heard about any visiting fair-based group offering this entertainment." She pets Ziggy while we talk.

I hate to do this as I know from past experience how much people who coordinate things do not like sudden changes or unauthorized things because of potential liability and other issues. I use my Cowardly Lion staff not to make her forget, no. I could never do a dementia spell because of what happened to my father. Instead, I cast a spell that will keep Laura from being able to talk about the "paint balling of the witches and wizards" activity or any of our other plans but just give out the fliers on it.

Ziggy whispers via the R.U.S.E., doing a puppy whine but trying to be brave, "Please do not make me change the things I say."

"It had to be done in this case," I inform him, "I could not think of anything else to keep her from telling and ruining our plan." This seems to satisfy him.

With this, I head to the van and circus trailer where I walk the chicken-legged trailer. People stare at it along the way.

I hand them the flier that mentions the audio-animatronic/robotic witches and wizards.

"More robotics, folks... just more amazing robotics, folks," I state as I hand out more fliers, "Come one... come all at 3 p.m. at the fairgrounds to see this marvel and more and shoot yourselves some evil witches and wizards with some paintball guns!" I really do feel like great-great-great-great grandfather now back in his showman days with the hot-air balloon at the traveling carnivals in Nebraska.

I continue to walk the chicken-legged yellow trailer over to my circus trailer. Ziggy whispers via the R.U.S.E., "Boy what I would not do to get a hold of one those chicken legs!" I chuckle, and it eases my anxiety a little.

I create a second ball hitch on the back of the circus trailer itself and put the chicken legged trailer on it. The chicken legs finally re-ascend to a compartment within the trailer so that the yellow trailer can roll on wheels.

After I have done all of this, I state to the Cowardly Lion, "Thank you for your patience, my friend. We are going to need your help in the coming battle, and you're going to be a free, loose lion again."

The Cowardly Lion roars and says, "I am ready for battle, and I will meet those sons of witches and wicked wizards as they come!" And with this, in a flash of light, we teleport to the Ionia Fair Ground for last minute preparations for and the final Out World battle. I hope that once and for all many, many, curses, including Westy's, will be broken for good.

Chapter 14.7
Jeremiah's Journey

Man, I TOLD O.Z. DIGGS THAT I WOULD TAKE
care of getting the Headless Horseman costume in
Massachusetts, and that's what I did, though it took
a lot longer than I thought it would. My wife, Aurora
Strongs, a real beauty with blonde locks to the neck
and a winning smile, wanted to go with me. I
explained that a coven at least 417 years old was in
Salem, Massachusetts and that they feed upon
female energy and try to pull it into their fold.
Unfortunately, a few good witches from Oz and even
some local white witch mid-wives who dabbled in
herbs for healing were killed during the Salem Witch
Trials. However, this business about only benevolent
witches being around Salem, Massachusetts or
Massachusetts in general just is not true. Man, the
truly wicked are everywhere. All they really need is
love, man.

My wife relented and agreed to stay behind.
However, she sent her familiar, an emerald green
dragonfly from Oz to fly near me and watch over me

should I need additional help. He's a cute little booger.

She tended to believe that she could project her spirit there to the dragonfly, a kind of astral projection. Not only are we both mages, but we're old hippies you see. Why do you think I have had the long grey hair and beard for so long? Why do you think she tie-dyed her robes? -Fits, doesn't it, man?

She and I both knew that there was a dangerous warlock, the Rev. Bartholomew Abbot, who lived under many names in the Salem area through hundreds of years and hundreds of years before that in the British Isles and led the witches there. He, who was a dark wizard having been banned hundreds of years ago from Oz by Lurline Herself, was one of the ones who led the charge against witches during the Salem Witch Trials but purposefully sought out those benevolent witches from Oz and the local white witches to destroy. Though the Rev. Bartholomew Abbot, who always wears a dark suit and well-groomed, black slick hair to appear churchy, had an upper level degree in divinity, what some people did not know was that his monogram also stood for B.A., a B.A. in Dark Arts. He only read up more on the divine so that he could, with dark spirits, try to thwart the divine's efforts in this world. Aurora was right to be afraid for my safety. Woah.

I knew a lot about what he had done to some of the good wizards and witches who tried to bring him down over 200 years ago when they came here from Oz. There was a group of 30 powerful ones who were banding together to use their powers and their staffs against the Rev. Abbot, the warlock, before his witches could get to him to help.

The Rev. Abbot, using a staff of the darkest oak he procured from a tree blackened with blood where Celtic people had once been sacrificed by the Druids, called forth demons and spirits of the evil dead to help him in a transformation spell. This was not to transform himself but all 30 powerful, good wizards and witches.

There was an old mill near a stream and pond that was in a relatively remote area around Fitchburg or Worcester, Massachusetts. ("Down near the old mill stream..." man, "The Beatles should have done that barber shop one during their "Sergeant Pepper" period.) Anyway, the mill stream was frozen over that winter the aforementioned 30 good wizards and witches had come after him during the solstice. Using his transformation spell, the warlock Rev. Abbot turned all 30 into geese, enchanted them so that they would always be full and never die, and locked them into place in the frozen ice. He also waved his dark staff and made it so that they would be invisible to people during the winter and kept their honking from being unable to be heard. People near there would think that they had migrated further south for the winter. Isn't that a kicker?

The poor souls actually felt the frozen ice, though, but could never die. You would think that in the thaw that they would be okay, but no! This is the part that makes me want to urinate right on the Rev. Abbot's grave should he ever actually die on this earth, man. He made an illusion to the onlookers so that the good magic users would look like cavorting geese during the spring, summer, and fall in a picturesque scene but invisible during the winter, but in reality would be good magic users transformed into geese with their legs frozen in an enchanted stream year round. They still felt the freeze of the ice. Their geese bodies were never allowed to succumb to it completely. The enchanted

151

wizards and witches did not die as a result of it but were protected by dark magic so that they would continue in their suffering. -All because they tried to over-throw that bastard.

If Rev. Bartholomew Abbott, B.A. in Dark Arts, knew one of the co-leaders of the good wizards and witches of Oz was coming to Massachusetts, he would be sure to send his coven of Salem witches after them. I had to know what to expect. But as I was stepping foot in that wondrously weird state again just to get a Headless Horseman costume, I had to do all I could to help those poor tortured souls.

The place I teleported into was Lynn, Massachusetts at night but thankfully not quite the witching hour and at least some distance from Salem.

Before me stood a two story, wood-boarded structure that had its claim to fame as Massachusetts' oldest gay bar and several blocks from me loomed the sugary yet smoky-smelling Fluffery factory. The Fluffery factory made a kind of marshmallow spread that New Englanders loved on peanut butter sandwiches. My friend Oscar (O.Z. Diggs) would have loved them, but I never had much of a sweet tooth. Contrary to popular belief, those of us old hippies who... how shall I say... partake in the cannabis do not always get munchies for sweets. - Got it, man?

I had to ask where a really huge costume shop was. Your run of the mill penny ante shop probably was not going to have Headless Horseman, particularly as there was no Sleepy Hollow film that year.

When I walked in, there was a shiny bulbed platform as kind of a run-way stage in the center not far from the first bar. A man dressed all in a black pleather witch's outfit and with bright green make-up was singing a cover of "Little Girls" from Annie, cavorting to and fro.

"Some witches are covered with potions. Other witches' coverings are unfurled. Lucky me... lucky me... I'm just covered by a ... Kansas girl." Suddenly, hanging from a rafter, a handle of a bucket of water with a string attached to it which went off stage was tugged at via said string. A bucket of water fell on the non-magic-using drag queen. She started screaming, "My make-up's melting... melting... what has unfurled when an ugly twink can rid the world of my loveliness...melting...melting." She then shinnied out of her loose black robes and disappeared through a trap door making it look like she had melted. Man, oh, man.

Well, some witches, such as the ones in Salem, are so ancient that they are so dried out that throwing water on them will make them disintegrate. I do not think I have ever seen a man dressed as a witch acting this out, though.

The emerald dragonfly on my shoulder, my wife's familiar, whispered, "Ignore her. As you know, she's not a real witch. Go ask about the costume shop." I had almost forgotten the emerald dragonfly until I saw its resplendent wings and shiny verdant qualities as seen in the nearby dance floor lights. Being an old bearded man in grey robes that looked kind of like a dress with a dragonfly on my shoulder resembling costume jewelry just made me look like a very eccentric transvestite. Man, isn't that funny? You know that all of us hippies do get along with and love the gay folks. Come on now. But sometimes things are just funny. We all have to laugh at ourselves. We have forgotten how to do that, and all of us take ourselves too seriously, man.

I quickly found a young man to ask a question of. He had short hair and appeared to be in his twenties. He was dressed in fancy pants and shoes but wore a thrift store T-shirt with them to be trendy. The dragonfly on my shoulder whispered, "Here comes trouble."

I asked, "Do you know where the closest, biggest costume shop is?"

He turned around at me and stared. His eyes were so wide that I thought he might be on some sort of drug or could just be delusional in general. He said in a cracking voice, "I'm a thousand-year-old witch who has lived many past lives. I love going to Salem and-"

I stopped his magazine model cataloging of attributes right there, man, and slowly stepped away. The dragonfly whispered that she told me he would be trouble. When someone thinks they are a thousand-year-old witch from Salem and is not actually one, it's time to step away. Besides, he would have had to have been a Native American witch of some sort for that truly to be true. Man, if you're going to have a delusion, at least get your history straight or er, gay, in this case.

With the dragonfly on my shoulder's approval, I finally found a nice lesbian lady with short hair and a tank-top who told me that for an educational program where she works that they use a big costume shop in Fitchburg. That was not far from the old mill stream area I was talking about. I asked her about that, and she said that the old mill had been converted into a restaurant on the stream. I thanked her profusely and ran out to teleport.

But before I could, a huge bear-like creature but one that looked like it was made of peanut butter covering Fluffery, the marshmallow spread, approached. Anyway, it looked like a brown bear, man, which I knew were mostly out west and that black bears were in western Massachusetts and sometimes further east. It was drippy, though, as if it was made of wet clay, but it was the runny peanut butter on its outside that made it that way. The dripping qualities made it reveal its even softer interior of Fluffery. It was not a Powder of Life creature because it could not talk. It was just a blobby bear-like mess made partially from the local Fluffery factory and peanut butter factory with magic by the Rev. Bartholomew Abbott either to destroy me or to at least delay me while he did more.

The Fluffery nutty bear ran towards me with the speed of a regular bear. And if you know anything about bears as I do from my long years of camping, they are incredibly fast! We are talking line-backer on steroids fast, man!

Using my chalk-covered staff, I magically drew myself as a bear too. However, as the Fluffery nutty bear got closer, it just got my fur sticky and would have made me like Brer Rabbit with the Tar Baby.

I decided to turn myself into a Chihuahua. I had a Chihuahua at home and like Ziggy the Corgi, I have heard, liked to lick people to death. He liked to give people lots of licks to the face and hands.

Turning into a Chihuahua with my chalk-donned staff, I quickly licked and licked the Fluffery nutter bear. Soon, I had its outer layer of peanut butter taken care of. Man, I don't have much of a sweet tooth, but I do love the nutty roasted qualities of peanut butter. Now that's probably a stoner stereotype for ya!

The fake bear, not even truly alive as a Powder of Life creature, pantomimed opening its mouth to roar, but even that was fake.

I continued to lick and lick, dodging his big paws.

I knew that I would be way too sticky and possibly caught in his drippy mess if I was not quick. That is another reason I chose the Chihuahua. They can run like mini-Greyhounds when they want to – especially if they have been cooped up for a while.

I licked and licked and licked some more.

I had the Fluffery nutter bear down to its Fluffery, soft white marshmallow spread middle.

This I made quick work of by biting it away, and the fake brown bear, the non-alive bunch of peanut butter and goo was taken care of, and I transported to Fitchburg.

I quickly obtained the Headless Horseman costume at a shop there because I knew I would have to rush shortly after that... especially with what I was planning.

I teleported to the Old Mill Restaurant and made it so that the enchanted geese, the 30 good wizards and witches, could fly away, carrying part of the frozen stream with them. The Rev. Abbott sent his coven after us, witches flying on brooms. Flying the geese above the witches, I proceeded to make some of the ice the geese were carrying mid-air start to melt as if a cloud of sleet. The water began to fall upon the ancient witches, and they screamed, melting off of their broomsticks and dripping below in green goo the locals thought was pollution or acid rain. Man, that was heavy. Literally and figuratively!

Having destroyed so many with the elemental of water increased the power of my staff for a while and, honing in on the Rev. Abbott, I shot a beam of pure light toward his heart, destroying him once and for all. Malignant spirits carried off the tatters of his soul to a dark realm, and the geese were at peace at last.

I knew I better not transform them back yet, man, because they would need new staffs, could not teleport, and had a long way to go.

I turned to the dragonfly on my shoulder and asked, "Will you, like, do the honors?"

The dragonfly led the geese, who though wizards and witches still had geese-y instincts and wanted to catch the insect for food, on a wild dragonfly chase to and fro out west. I turned myself into one of the flock as well to help lead them, and we took the long migratory journey back to Ionia. Well, I sped it up with some magic. But we would soon be back to help O.Z. Diggs, man, and in spades or at least bills.

Chapter 15

Fair is "Fowl" and Foul is Fair for O.Z. Diggs VII

Upon TELEPORTING THE VAN, CIRCUS TRAILER, and trailer with chicken legs and all of my friends and me into the Ionia fairgrounds some distance from the Tesla coils on the spiral-topped whimsical gate edges, I rush a little to the Tesla coils and make short work of them. I blow both of them out with my staff. Then, with a gigantic roar from my Cowardly Lion staff, I blast the gates open. I am so focused that I ignore the Ferris wheel, a rollercoaster, carousel, funhouse, and house of horrors left behind by a small carnival company when Catie Sheeney, possessed with Mombi, drove the carnies out with evil magic. I gaze at the attractions a minute.

While I have done this, Jeremiah Strongs III has appeared through a chalk portal in his Headless Horseman attire and his hugging him wife Aurora who recognizes his voice through it.

Aurora states that Jeremiah has asked that we use our staffs to un-enchant the geese flying above. She pets a dragonfly on her arm gingerly. "Nice work, my pet," she says to it.

We have the geese land. Aurora says that Jeremiah told her through the costume (his head is not visible in it after all) that the ice they were enchanted in melted the rest of the journey.

We then focus our staffs on the geese. They become various wizards and witches, and we send them to procure new staffs for the upcoming battle. They thank us all profusely, but we say there is not much time for congratulations but do say they are very welcome, that we were happy to help them.

We do not say much because of the urgency. I affix the hag face jug to the Headless Horseman costume and enchant it with my staff to make funny faces and look here and there. The hag jug will also mutter from now on. From a distance, Jeremiah will look like a powerful, tall hag. I tell him that I may need him immediately for the battle but will let him know momentarily. I think of something else.

From my bag, I pull out the witch's hat and the leather robe with the red stitches I picked up after we destroyed that rebel evil witch at the land bridge zoo in Pennsylvania. I put this symbolic attire of the evil rebels atop my friend's Headless Horseman disguise and moving expression face jug respectively. There is so much to finalize with the last-minute details of the plan. Thank goodness we were able to get more magic reinforcements thanks to Jeremiah's help in Massachusetts.

Thinking of the impending run-in with the wicked witches and evil warlocks who may be coming their way from the Mombi-possessed poultry barn head-quarters, I cast a slow-down spell. I do not want to freeze them in time completely but just buy us some time for the strategies for their defeat.

I quickly release the Cowardly Lion from the circus trailer, who via the nearby R.U.S.E. on Ziggy states so that we can understand it, "ROAR! I will make short work of these wicked ones! Bring 'em my way!" The flier did state that a tame lion would be released on the premises. I hope people pay attention to that part. The R.U.S.E. translates for the Cowardly Lion and Ziggy only when the Outworldians are not around. We have to be careful.

I have put Ziggy's shiny silver armor on the friendly Corgi, and his snout cover that it at once sword and shield in one sparkles with its diamond and prismatic tip. The hinges on it still work quite well and allow him to be chatty as always. I have placed a protective cup with holes in and have magically affixed it to Ziggy so that our ovate amber snail friend, R.U.S.E., will have a place to translate from for those in the know about the talking animals and be protected.

Ziggy says, "I still struggle with worry over battle as my anxiety rune indicates, but I will be valorous as that rune on my dog tag indicates!"

The Cowardly Lion states that being worried does not make one a coward but facing up to things makes one a lot more than a coward.

As they talk, I am busily replicating the eggs from the chicken trailer I brought with me and replicating the yo-yos and the cork guns (clones of Catie Sheeney's childhood's Soldier with the Green Whiskers Oz collectible cork gun). I have Jeremiah and the other good 50-100 wizard of witches of the Society of the Walking Cane, who soon join us to a little brief fanfare but not enough pomp and circumstance to get in the way. I set them to work pouring blessed wine from the cathedral in Syracuse over the many corks we got in Peekskill, which I have also replicated. We had the corks from theses bottles themselves to the stockpile.

Even the R.U.S.E. is let out of his protective cup for a while and uses a small dish of wine that he is careful and brave not to spill on himself and his slimy arms and hands the elves bestowed him with. The R.U.S.E. generally dips one cork at a time into the wine and lays it aside. The corks take up a good part of the majority of his body, and I admire this bravery. As per the Society of the Walking Cane, we do not mention that in their presence that I have not had to state who I am. The curse seems to have been lifted.

I have enchanted the chicken trailer to scratch evil wizards and wicked witches who come near it, to jump up, land on them like the house landed on the Wicked Witch of the East and scratch the heck out of them until they retreat. As many are practically dust themselves, this may destroy them. The spell I used was one I felt powerful enough to cast after my week or more of practice after becoming a truly powerful wizard by facing the trials of the elementals, earth, fire, and water. What has made me especially powerful as a benevolent Wizard is communing with God in different forms. Baba Yaga will be incensed when she finds out what I have done to her chicken trailer with my powers. It will take several of us to take her down. At least, I anticipate that it will.

Replicating the eggs has taken at least 20 minutes as preparing the corks with the wine has had for the Society members, and I have to make the egg-yos. I quickly blast the eggs and the Oz souvenir yo-yos (cloned from Catie's childhood, part of a guilt bribe as her father left her) with a spell to combine them, making kind of elliptical unbroken yet roundly

161

flattened eggs on either side of the yo-yo strings. The eggs can break when one extends them out with the yo-yo string and will be needed for if and when the Nomes come. More can be made in the poultry barn if we can ever get to it. The good wizard and witches and even Outworldians can use the yo-yos as weapons. Like people in Oz, they can also use eggs as weapons at the very same time.

All of this rushed preparation has taken 40 minutes at least at this point, and festival crowds are starting to drive through the gates to the parking area. As the Out Wordlians come with the paint ball flier, the plan is to hand them each a cork-gun with a handful of cork ammo dipped with holy sacramental blessed wine to the point of absorption. The Outworldians understand perfectly what they are to do with they see the "audio-animatronic"/ "so realistic" wicked witches and evil warlocks.

Though I did cast the slow down spell on the wicked witches and evil warlocks, they are finally approaching many feet down from the poultry headquarters. They pass down the midway where all the abandoned fair rides are. They walk as slowly as zombies or people with leg pain and are mostly dressed in the darkest ebony with pointy hats here and there. They have the strange red ancient symbols on their black leather robes as well. My slow down spell will not last forever, and I will need to concentrate on efforts to blast the evil ones with my Cowardly Lion staff along with the members of the Society of the Walking Cane.

The R.U.S.E. says, "They really are moving at a snail's pace, and I of all creatures can say that."

We laugh with a bit of nervous laughter. The septuagenarian members from the smooth-faced and colored-hair that betrayed their ancient qualities to the truly old looking laughed what could only be described as a crowd laugh of about one hundred in unison. Clean, good living kept them youthful and joyful. But they grew silent quickly with respect when they saw who approached.

An elderly female good witch in the Society of the Walking Cane with short hair and glasses who had once been a primary school teacher, carries an Old School whacking cane from the early years of the public-school system which doubles as her staff and walking cane. She reminds me of Locasta, the Good Witch of the North. In fact, she is the descendant of Locasta. However, she has been able to go back, using her good witch powers, to Oz and return from time to time. She herself is Locasta VII, but she does not have the curse I have.

She yells, knowing about his disguise, "Jeremiah, let's give them a few raps of the old cane and send them to their corner of hell, dunce caps and all!" She pointed to the tall, dark hats many of them insisted on wearing.

The Cowardly Lion roars, "I will pounce them straight to where the goblins go!" (I ask Jeremiah Strongs III, who is equally enthusiastic) to hide in his disguise as the strong, tall hag and appear in a flash theatrically during the battle right in front of Cattie.

"I may be meek at times," Ziggy states, "But I am one heck of a warrior and can nudge their calves with this sword-shield on my snout to the point that they will hit the earth. Hopefully, the elves will open up a big hole in it to swallow them up!"

"I will gladly continue to translate all of this trash talk from the animals here!" states the R.U.S.E., "And will help with communications from the animals to the humans!"

"Wow," says one of the bespectacled Outworldians who has approached with what he thinks is a paintball gun to shoot audio-animatronic figures. He has not heard the translation but is just marveling at the sights around him. A crowd of at least 50-100 or more behind him gasp and make equal statements. "How real!", "How do they do that?", "This is exciting", and a lot of other comparable statements are made by the Outworldian crowd armed with the cork guns with the sacramental wine corks. They are asked to leave their egg-yos in a row in a field to retrieve later but keep their armed cork guns with extra evil deterrent ammunition. I learned how to set up equipment when I did games in addition to my storytelling sessions at youth events. As a wizard, though, I have learned to cast strong protective spells on stuff I do not want messed with. This is what I did here with the egg-yos.

Together, the Outworldians and the Society of the Walking Cane Ozians make an army of approximately 200 individuals to battle against the 300 evil witches and warlocks who have shared travel trailers and recreational vehicles in downtown Ionia. The numbers of evil always exceed the good. Hundreds of evil nomes may be on their way too. Our small rag-tag army through faith, hope, love for each other, and magic can defeat these malignant masses. I am sure of it.

Many of the Outworldians recognize me. They identify me as the Wizard of Oz because of my wizard hat, emerald green glasses, emerald coat, and Cowardly Lion staff. Many of them do recognize me as my great-great-great-great grandfather or at least having a connection to him. This is enough to work against Westy's weakened curse. The Society of the Walking Cane recognize me too. I do not have to introduce myself as O.Z. Diggs the Seventh any more. Now that the curse is broken, I can travel to

Oz once this final Out World battle is over. The wicked ones approaching do not know this, and I do not plan on telling them. They are not quite close enough to hear what I am saying to the about 200-person army. Not all of the Society of the Stitches may know through word of mouth or even through Mombi that my curse is now broken.

Like my politician great-great-great-great grandfather before me but in a more modern way, I give a mini stump speech, "I am Oz the Great and Terrible wizard, seventh heir to the wizarding part of Oz! These wicked witches and evil wizards are taking over this area and are keeping many wonderful things from happening and keeping many from fulfilling what they need to do. Have at them and make short work of them! There is no help for them! I am the next Wizard of Oz, and I approve this carnage!"

And with this, the evil warlocks and wicked witches have reached us, worrying me little or no if they have heard my speech at this point, and the first part of the final Out World battle ensues.

Chapter 15.7

It Did Not Locasta Much

I WAS NAMED AFTER MY ANCESTOR, AND I AM Locasta VII, a primary school teacher-esque sweet lady yet a force to be reckoned with if you cross me. I took it upon myself some time before this Great Out World Battle that has happened in Ionia, Michigan to venture to California.

There, they had an Anti-Diggs-convention (an Anti-Diggs-con) somewhere between San Diego and Los Angeles, and they were in a fancy hotel not far from some cliffs and those awful little hills full of brush that they call mountains there (not the Sierra Nevada...those are lovely... I am talking about those dried-up little hills with chasms around them where they put expensive houses).

The Anti-Diggs evil witches and wizards who convened there were part of the ones who had been thrown out of Oz. They convened to circulate only the classic L. Frank Baum and Ruth Plumly Thompson takes on the O.Z. Digg's story. They did not want anybody ever writing that the first O.Z.

Diggs was married or had children. To them, he was a confirmed bachelor and would stay that way.

The L. Frank Baum tales are lovely, and he was our greatest historian. The Anti-Diggs-con folks have grown to focus more on Baum as a historian and not a passer-on of tales from our magical malleable fairy world of Oz. They try to reign his books and other story-tellers' works with strict rules when he himself broke them. He contradicted himself and embellished things here and there. That was all part of the wonder of Oz. And some of them focus on Thompson more as a historian not because they love Oz and its fantastic aspects but so that they can find out some obscure, minor facet about Oz from her and hold it over others' heads. This obsession by the Anti-Digg-ites kept the focus off of the new stories of Oz and how O.Z. Diggs VII was really a part of American society and wanted to return to Oz.

The reason they wanted it kept that way was so that O.Z. Diggs VII could never return to help his ancestor in fighting off the evil up-rising of malignant witches and wizards that had started there, those in the leathery black robes with the red stitching.

They may have sensed that I was coming through one of my magic puffs of chalk dust teleportation (a technique my ancestor taught me), but they did not see me as a threat. After all, what could one good person or good witch do who wanted to make a difference in the world? What could she do against an entire evil group? Particularly a little old kind lady, they thought.

Do not judge me by my grey curly perm. Confuse not the twinkle in my eye for kindness for all. I am kind to those who are willing to change. I am kind to those who do not choose to stay evil.

Choose to stay, evil, though, and I will summon all the benevolent power at my grasp to rid the earth of you.

Anyway, the anti-Diggs-con folks made sure to distribute the original stories of L. Frank Baum and Ruth Plumly Thompson, which are excellent by the way (particularly the original L. Frank Baum ones) but not in the way they were using them. They also passed out literature to those interested in the occult about their dark magic practices at the con. There was even a table full of occult merchandise coupled with the dark arts. And this from some of the anti-Diggs folks who thought that God and beliefs should never figure into Oz – even through Lurline, the Fairy Creator. The anti-Diggs con became a kind of dark magic and purist Oz con all in one.

The convention hall was full of all of them giving presentations on obscure topics such as a duck character from a book further in the series or another minor character here or there. It made these people feel great if they could find the most obscure nugget of information about a character in the later books that not many knew about – particularly if it was one from one of Thompson's books. All of this created additional distraction from the true story of O.Z. Diggs VII and why he was in the United States.

What they did not know was that in addition to learning my ancestor's techniques with the prognosticating slate and chalk and teleporting with chalk dust, I had a few proverbial tricks up my sleeve as well. Seeing my ancestor's eraser, I made a magic trick of my own. I could use my grandmother's old chalkboard eraser to erase anything in reality in real time.

Anyway, I knew that on one of those dirty, scraggly little mountains that they have there in that area, that an over-expensive tiny house, a second or third home of a starlet that she did not really need, was being moved from the hilly, cavernous area to the shore. It was being moved by helicopter on steel cables and was scheduled to fly over the Anti-Diggs Convention Hall that very afternoon.

I waited in an over-grown garden area with rose bushes and topiaries not far from the convention hall. I would have to be quick with the eraser. I might be killed.

I saw the tiny house being transported with cables was approached. "Oh, dear, they ought not fly that too close," I stated in my voice which most say is very sweet and grandmotherly. My voice did drip a bit with sarcasm at the end.

As soon as the helicopter was flying overhead, I teleported my magic chalkboard eraser to the cables holding the tiny house.

"What a mess has been made here," I stated again like an old fuss-budget, "I think it's time to clean it up!"

My magic eraser then did its work!

"Oh, dear, look what I've done," I murmured, holding a white-gloved hand to my mouth.

Not even a ping or clang noise ensued from the cables, that's how clean of an erasure happened. Gravity then took over, and I could hear the whoosh noise as the tiny house fell. SPLAT!

The tiny house fell on the entire convention hall, and at least this particular group of wicked witches and wicked wizards were dead. I dusted off my hands of chalk-dust and looked at the hotel.

I said, pulling a strand of grey hair off of my forehead, "This hotel is...clean."

I meant clean spiritually at the moment but looking at the debris from the wrecked convention hall, the over one hundred piles of dust that the ancient dried out evil hags and wizards became upon being crushed, I stated, "Oh, dear...they certainly are going to have a hard time cleaning all of that up." It would be quite the Herculean task in that stable of former jackasses.

Some members of the resort hotel staff rushed out. One stated, "Thank goodness no one was in there. No signs of bodies."

"We could have had a lawsuit on our hands even though it was not our fault," said one of the managers.

"Just dust it off your shoulders and shoes, boys," I say, walking away with my disciplinary rod staff, "Just dust it off." They nod and look a little perplexed.

Then, I laugh to myself, singing, in this case, 'CLING-CLANG...the witches are dead!" once I am out of ear-shot.

Well, and wicked wizards too.

This task having been done, I had teleported in a cloud of chalk-dust to Ionia, Michigan to join the ensuing battle that was happening there.

Chapter 16

Heading Toward a "Poultry" Existence and the Phony Fair

THE OUTWORLDIANS START SHOOTING THE corks at the wicked witches and evil warlocks. "Ayeeeeeeeeeee!" they scream when the cork with the holy, blessed wine hits their skin (we tell the Out World folks to aim for the face for direct skin contact for the holy wine absorbed in the cork).

They then shrivel up, leaving just black robes with odd, red symbols behind.

A young man says, "Cool...that's so real. Realer than the local paintball place."

"Realer than theme park effects" states a kid.

A military adult states, "That's even more real than the paintball training we did to simulate combat at times."

They continue to shoot their doctored cork guns toward the evil foes.

The Cowardly Lion pounces on a few of the ancient evil witches and wizards here and there, and they turn to puffs of dust, leaving dusty ebony clothes behind. He roars as he goes through battle, having been afraid of wicked witches in the past but not showing it now. Again, the Out Wordlians stare in wonder at the special effects being used to make it look like the lion is destroying the wicked witches and evil warlocks. "Cowardly" makes short work of the evil ones. We explain to the visitors that this is all part of a trained lion act for the fair.

Ziggy, with his crystal diamond tipped nose-piece, infused with elven magic, nudges and trips many as he practices his typical Corgi herding behavior, circling the group of evil ones with little quick feet. If the metal part of his snout shield bangs against their ankles and calves as he nudges his strong snout toward them, many of the evil ones trip and are vanquished through our weapons. Direct magic elven crystal diamond contact with their skin, particularly if the sun shines through it, causes the wicked ones to shrivel up.

The Society of the Walking Cane and I explain to Outworldians that we are testing laser guns disguised as staffs which when hitting the right target makes the witches disappear through green screen technology.

At least 200 evil witches and wizards are hit by the Outworldians doctored cork guns and our magic staffs. This is all in the course of about two hours.

The Society of the Walking Cane manages to prevent any Outworldians from getting injured but suffer from gashes here and there. Thankfully, few of the gashes seem fatal if at all, and no members of the Society have been expired.

The rest of the wicked witches and wizards, about 100 of them, retreat toward the fair rides, and it looks like some of them are entering them. About 33 of them line up in the metal queue bars of the carousel, 33 at the haunted house, and 33 at the funhouse. They enter quickly through the turn-styles like smug teenagers ignoring carnies' instructions. They skip the Ferris wheel where they would be as much shooting ducks as the ones in the shooting gallery in the games areas. This was no time for a day at the fair, but I knew they had other plans in mind. In this case, fair really is foul.

I also wonder where in the world Baba Yaga is, but I am not able to concentrate on that much.

I announce to the folks, "We are testing having the robots ride on rides with folks. I hope you have enjoyed your free preview session of the wicked witch and evil wizard paintball experience! I also hope you continue to enjoy the Wizard of Oz festival Ionia. Do not forget to go to the classic 1920s cinema and for this weekend only pay the 1939 price for Wizard of Oz tickets, a quarter apiece!"

The Out-world residents applaud and head toward their cars. I want to spare them of what Mombi has in mind. I am very grateful for them helping. We could not have done it without them. I forget for a while that we may need them later.

And, yes, quite a few of them thought I was connected to or was the real O.Z. Diggs and started talking about how the wicked witches and the evil warlocks were actually real and that the Society of the Walking Cane, the Outworldians, and I were engaged in a real battle. Some were shushed. Others were listened to. The belief in who I was saying I actually was strengthened me even further. Old Westy's curse definitely is not having any control of me now.

I tell the Outworldians good-bye, and I rush with the Society of the Walking Cane and my animal friends to the fair equipment.

The Cowardly Lion goes in the haunted house with some of the Society members. He scratches and pounces at both fake and real witches within the haunted house while the Society members use their staffs to reveal who the real evil witches and warlocks are amongst the cheesy haunted house décor. Bloody fake limbs and fake blood dominate the settings of mostly asylum cells, labs, and haunted house rooms. A stick with a stuffed green witch on it would move forward via hydraulics when their ride cars passed by. Cowardly swipes it, I have heard from somebody who comes out of the ride and takes no chances. Cowardly pounces on all of the wicked witches and evil wizards who dare jump from the shadows of the haunted house. They quickly dwindle in number and become less and less scary and comparable to the cheesy effects with their jumping out and scratching hands. Of the 100 left, 33 wicked witches and wizard incognito as equally evil horror movie witches and wizards are vanquished within the haunted house.

The next group of 33 wicked witches and evil warlocks on the carousel does not do some cliché thing of making the horses come off the carousel and gallop. Instead, they magically pop the fiberglass-tent-like top off of the carousel off the top of it and float the entire bottom apparatus with the horses in their circle. They collectively make it magically go through up past where the top of the carousel used to be and descend toward Ziggy with Ziggy toward the middle of the circle, where a cylinder used to be when the bottom circle of the carousel was in its proper place. With this bottom circle of carousel horses, these 33 members of the Society of the Stitches have Ziggy and a few members of the Society of the Walking Cane trapped and start magically speeding up the bottom circle part with the horses they ride over and over again. Ziggy can deftly circle too as a breed raised to herd and circle. He circles in the inner circle as the outer circle of carousel horses continues. His stubby little paws surprisingly have him moving excessively fast. He is agile and strong.

Ziggy states, via the R.U.S.E. to only the Society members, "Sometimes... yes... pant... yes... pant... a little force is necessary to keep the herd in line."

He jumps up with all his might on the spinning circle with the carousel horses and with his strong diamond and crystal tipped snout shield clangs against the horses and knocks them down. The Society members do the same with their cane staffs.

As the dried-out witches have fallen and have nearly crumbled to dust, Ziggy urinates on a few causing them to melt completely. Many of these were vile, child-killing witches, so Ziggy feels no guilt in doing this, he says.

Some of the wizards get the same treatment, and others are vanquished with staffs. Ziggy destroys still others with his shield-sword on his snout by contacting the elven magic crystal diamond to their skin.

The R.U.S.E. even helps by creating a bit of a, well, ruse by throwing the wicked witch's and evil warlocks' voices he is interpreting from the ground where they sit, changing messages to sew miscommunication between the enemy. The snail does a bit of sound espionage.

A few of this group of 33 wicked witches and evil warlocks evade being wet by Ziggy or hit by his magic snout shield. Still others evade the staffs of the Society of the Walking Cane.

They are about to retreat when the group of members of the Society of the Walking Cane join hands and focus their walking cane staffs toward the ring of horses. They cause it to rise and then fall on the rest of the evil witches and wizards in this section. They disintegrate to dust.

"Now, be gone before somebody drops a carousel on you too," the former schoolteacher good witch yells to the remaining ones in the funhouse, where we are just able to get in through automated processes after I have started the equipment. I have been able to see what has transpired or have heard about what has transpired at the other two fair locations through the power of my staff. Amazing.

I also observe the darker and hot colored carousel horses, looking like Death's and even Underworld horses, grabbing the spirits of the deceased wicked witches and evil warlocks.

The Society of the Walking Cane members near the carousel practice something they will need to do later.

They all grab hands, pray to Lurline (one of the forms of God), and focus their staffs toward the ground, opening up a chasm to the Underworld. They are practicing because they know they will need to do this with the spirit of Mombi later. Thankfully, I have an intense plan for that.

The darker and hot colored carousel horses grab the spirits of the deceased and rush them toward the chasm.

Ziggy says, "Now that's the horses of a different 'mauler' I've heard tell about."

The Society laughs with him for just a moment but then look very grave and very old as they ponder the wicked ones going to the afterlife.

The wicked ones scream blood curdling screams as they go through the chasm to their fates.

The Society of the Walking Cane quickly close up the chasm, and those particular wicked witches and wizards are seen no more.

Which just leaves me and a few other members in the walk-through Funhouse, trying to get rid of the remaining 33.

The evil ones do not use the mirrors in the funhouse to create fake versions of themselves. They do not lead me to "reflect on" who is real and who is a mirror image. That would be too banal for them.

Instead, they make portals of the fun-house mirrors from the ones that stretch one's image to great heights to the ones that make one appear squatty. The Queen of Hearts from Wonderland, a country Oz has had many dealings with according to some fantastic tales, sticks her arm out of an elongated one and tries to grab us as do heart cards. They do so through the Looking Glass on their end. They need the space of the elongated one on our end.

"Off with their heads," I hear shouted through the fun house mirrors which also cause the traditional trouble of not knowing how to get out of the funhouse maze.

A warlock's arm from the Land of Zo, a country that mirrors Oz but in reverse and in a culture that is completely different, comes through with fine silks and tries to grab us as well through a funhouse mirror that makes us appear squatty.

I know the evil wizard and witches here are not faking being mirror images themselves, so I quickly determine that they are behind the mirrors that are being enchanted as portals in real time. I can hear them muttering and giggling lightly behind the mirrors at times.

I blast these mirrors that are portals with my Cowardly Lion staff and ask the members of the Society of the Walking cane to do the same.

177

A superstitious little person codger (perhaps originally from Munchkin land) and a very tall person (perhaps from Gilliken country) both state, "But that's seven years back luck for each one!"

I state, "Ah...but you forget...in Oz, a little-known magic rule is that breaking a mirror removes seven years of regrets!"

Speaking of which, I also know that mirrors can be used magically to show internal regrets. I have hoped the wicked ones would not use this particular magic cliché after they did not replicate themselves, but they do.

I am shown as a hick from Boone, North Carolina in one of the mirrors. I keep walking and yell, "I am so much more than that!" I destroy that mirror and the person behind it with magic.

Yet another image shows my rainbow-colored hair and makes me out to be even more stereo-typically effeminate than I am. "I am not defined only by my sexuality but am not ashamed of it! I do not see it that way!" I scream. I continue. The other members of the Society have to face their demons of past self-hatred too so to speak. I destroy my particular mirror and ask that they do the same with theirs.

Shards of mirrored glass make strange colored patterns on the floor.

A final test comes to me. This one shows me aged about at the age that my great-great-great-great grandfather stopped aging at when he returned to Oz. I assert, "I love being a part of this magical family and do admire the traits I have like him. However, I am not my ancestor. I am me." I feel some pent-up anger at our ancestor putting us in this mess but bury it deep inside. With more rage than toward the other funhouse mirror, with the Cowardly Lion staff not roaring but glowing with red eyes, I destroy this mirror as well.

These 33 wicked witch and wizards' mirrored trickery is foiled.

We exit the funhouse. Nearly all of the remaining 100 Ozian evil witches and wizards in the Out World have been vanquished, and we rejoice.

One sniveling coward of an evil warlock, a bulbous man who barely fits in his black robe, goes running off to warn Catie Sheeney and therefore, the spirit of Mombi, and we cannot stop him.

We follow him toward the poultry center. I whistle for the trailer with the chicken legs to come with us. We will need him for if and when the Nomes come.

I then think back to those fliers that were circulated. I had dismissed the Outworldians. I had planned for them to have the egg-yos and help us while we used our staffs should the Nomes show up.

It was now five o'clock and the automatic generator-energized purple, red, and yellow vibrant lights of the fair glowed as much as the sun had just before dusk.

Using my Cowardly Lion staff, I change the writing on the front of the fliers still being circulated at the event in downtown and even place it on the backs of ones people already had. I put a curiosity spell into the fliers too. The ink of the fliers has a curiosity potion in it now.

"The Hatchin' Yo-yo Corporation invites youth of all ages to come out to the Ionia Fairground near the poultry area of the agricultural center to demonstrate the new egg-yos, novelty egg yo-yo pranks. People in nome costumes (I used the Outworld spelling of nome) will be here for you to demonstrate the prank of. Leave somebody with egg on their face! 6 p.m. tonight... the evening of the festival."

The fliers begin to work their magic, and I even put in an enticement spell on them for good measure.

With this having been done, the Society of the Walking Cane, the Cowardly Lion, Ziggy, the R.U.S.E., and I head to the gigantic red barn that houses the chicken coops at the poultry section of the Ag. Center of the Fair Grounds. I smell the earthy odor of hay and the faint odor of old animal excrement as we approach. It reminds me of areas back home.

Jeremiah Strongs is not far behind us, looking like a tall, green-faced strong hag with the Headless Horseman costume with the stringy-haired, ugly face jug atop it continuing to appear to mutter through my previously casted magic spell. Jeremiah has been tip-toeing behind buildings and rides incognito as the tall hag with the faux face. He has even used his chalk staff to make himself invisible at times. Jeremiah knows that if this plan we have is going to work that it will have to be a surprise.

I sigh as I think of the two messes that await us and not from the chickens, the mess of Catie Sheeney and the one who possesses her.

Chapter 17

**In Times of Trouble, Mother Mombi Comes
to Her**

W HEN THE SOCIETY OF THE WALKING CANE,
the Cowardly Lion, Ziggy and the R.U.S.E., and I
enter the poultry barn, we see it is full to the haylofts
with chicken coop after chicken coop. Hens of all
varieties, including the black and white Hamburg
variety that Oz chronicler L. Frank Baum raised, sit
and lay eggs. Cartons upon cartons of them, the eggs,
are off to the sides.

At the far end of the barn, in front of the last
sniveling evil warlock who has collapsed behind her
because of his failure, sits Catie Sheeney on a stool
using a singing sewing machine, a machine Mombi,
through her, has brought to life with Powder of Life.
(Mombi has killed the male messenger who came to
warn her (for his and the others' incompetence
presumably) and is adamantly and quickly pursuing
her plans.) The singing magic sewing machine is
labeled "Sue Eng Ma Shing." Sue Shing sings as she
stitches red patterns on leather robes for the spirit of

Mombi inside Catie Sheeney. Sue's mouth is on her sewing machine front along with two eyes and her mouth is nowhere near the bobbin as she sings, "I sew. I sew. Hours of work to go. La-la-la-la-la-la-la-la. I sew. I sew. I sew. I sew."

Mombi through Catie screeches, "She's not much of a SINGER!"

Catie in her monotone allows her own voice to be used and says, doing a Baumian joke, "She's sew-sew."

"Shut up, girl!" screeches Mombi.

I wave my Cowardly Lion staff and can see that the red symbols being stitched into the black robes (something that I never stopped to see before because of being in such of a rush) state via magic translation things like, "HATE DIGGS! HATE FRIENDS OF DIGGS! KILL ALL DIGGS! RISE AGAINST DIGGS!"

I yell, "You made them turn against my family and friends!"

Mombi states through Catie says, patting the mess of choppy ginger hair atop Catie's head in a girlish way, "Oh, you flatter me. I was never powerful enough to turn them against your family. You see... they already hated your family, those who joined the Society of the Stitches. I just played upon their hate, and the robes magically kept them that way."

I thought of the black robes with the red emblems left behind on the fairgrounds where we and the Outworldians had killed the wicked witches and the warlocks.

I turn to my friends and say, "The Nomes that are coming... they're going to be controlled by the black robes with the red emblems that were left behind! They're going to be controlled by the new ones!"

"That's right!" screams Mombi through Catie, "They're going to be controlled by me! The Nomes, controlled by red stitches, are going to get dear Catie and I everything we have ever wanted! The Society of the Stitches members were expendable as far as I was concerned!"

"You must have controlled O.Z. Diggs the First those years ago. You used this same kind of magic control on him somehow to have him bring you the baby Ozma," I say, trembling. I have wanted to know the answer to this for a long time.

The Society of the Walking Cane members lean in inquisitively on their staffs of all shapes, sizes, and colors of wood with varied designs that suit them.

Mombi through Catie stands and states, about to lift her wand, "I suppose it does not matter now... now that you are about to die."

The hag Baba Yaga, an ugly ogress, comes from behind a coop with her wand as well. Her chicken trailer has followed behind us through the huge barn doors that open out. She calls to it, and it does not come, and she screams, her mouth full of rotting teeth beneath her bulbous ogress nose, "What have you done to my precious pet?!"

"Now!" I scream to the chicken trailer, asking it to operate according to the spell casted on it by me in downtown Ionia. It jumps and starts scratching mid-air and lands squarely on Baba Yaga. A pair of curled Russian red shoes stick out beneath the chicken trailer. The chicken trailer immediately begins laying eggs.

Ziggy says, "It appears that she was a paper Yaga."

The Cowardly Lion asks, "Don't you mean paper tiger?"

"No," says the R.U.S.E. wincing slimily, "He meant the pun. And it appeared Baba Yaga's big pet... um, laid a few eggs." The R.U.S.E. laughs a little laugh. We roll our eyes but try to laugh. Things are just very stressful now. Plus, the pun was not that funny.

Mombi within Catie is truly furious now that she has lost Baba Yaga and the chicken trailer but speaks in a hushed tone with a deadpan gravitas that is creepier than her screeching, "It does not matter. You have killed the strongest one in my army so far, but it does not matter. I will kill you myself... and yes, I will let you know what happened with your great-great-great-great grandfather to cause him to bring Ozma to me. You see, the ancient Nome King Ruggedo was going to turn Princess Ozma into an object and take over all of Oz. He knew Oz would go into chaos once the fairy princess and heir of Pastoria was gone. O.Z. Diggs the First found out about this and had me turn Ozma into the boy Tip and asked me to hide her away." (Mombi does not know the Out World trope or really cliché of villains giving away too much of their plan to heroes because they think they are killing said heroes anyway, proving it pointless. She thinks she is doing something extra-ordinarily new and evil by telling me all this before my potential demise. She does not think there is any chance I will survive.)

I exclaim, "I knew my ancestor had a reason! I knew he would not have done something so evil!"

Mombi drones on, rolling her, well Catie's red eye-shadowed, eyes, "He continued to take over the throne until he could figure out what to do, having much to deal with when the Wicked Witches of the West and East took over. I had my day in the dark when I was the Wicked Witch of the North and had lived for hundreds of years by the time he approached me. I thought essentially being Ozma's kidnapper might benefit me one day. I bided my time. Once Tip escaped from me and learned he was really Princess Ozma incognito, not long after, I took the long journey to Ruggedo to inform him of the subterfuge. I told him and many others that the Wizard had hidden her away to usurp power and had forced me to keep Ozma hidden but that she was back in power nonetheless about 12 or so years after she was brought to me. I knew I would have a powerful friend in Ruggedo and asked many, many favors of him later as you know. Knowing will not help you now, though, because... you... die."

With this, Mombi through Catie reaches back to destroy me with her wand. Confident, I taunt the spirit of Mombi after her information dump with, "With that info. dump, have you been eating too much elven rune soup?" Crudoo's old crass humor calms me a minute. I distract Mombi with the non-sensical thought.

I shoot a few corks with the holy wine on them toward the body of Catie while a confused look graces her face.

Mombi screeches through her, "Nooooo! It feels like fire! Like fire!"

I state, "Catie... Catie, through the power of God and Christ, drive her out!"

Catie begins to gain more control. She has been second-guessing Mombi since our confrontation in Syracuse. She has been questioning the control Mombi has had over her since our confrontation in the cathedral. Mombi was weakened earlier in the cathedral too.

Catie's arm hovers mid-air. Her arm begins to shake and does not thrust forward.

"WEAK GIRL!" screeches Mombi through her, Catie's mouth, "you repugnant babyish girl with all your toys and your greed for more! WEAK BITCH! WEAK AS WATER FOR A NON-WITCH!"

Catie fights Mombi even further at this, remembering the way her mother spoke to her when her father left (she tells me this shortly thereafter while we are awaiting the arrival of the Nomes). They were able to cash in a large insurance policy through a missing person's clause and her father being declared legally dead. They climbed to the status of the wealthy. Catie's mom was always needling her about her many purchases. They had thousands to burn, and Catie had ran through a lot of it. However, Catie still did not deserve to be verbally abused.

I think of my own out-spoken mother and how supportive she was when it came to my story-telling and everything I had always tried. It seemed a sharp contrast to the way Catie was treated. Yet I had been through some hard times myself with what I went through with my father. He and I fought over who I wanted to be, but I grew out of my anger toward him for it. Catie turning to evil was not excused by her not being treated poorly when she was growing up. It never is in my opinion.

I think of Catie's need for toys and collectibles, her regressive tendencies. I have some of those myself at times, so I do understand. I go through my bag for the yellow bricks I have gleaned for her, have basically created.

I hurl them at her feet, trying not to hit her.

Catie says in her own monotone voice but softer, running her fingers through her choppy ginger locks as she looks through the bag, "You did this for me? You remembered that I wanted a yellow brick from the original one in Peekskill? The Land of Oz theme-park too?"

"Of course, he remembers," screeches Mombi through Catie's open mouth, "He is manipulating you, you weak girl!"

"It's true... I did want to use them to convince you in some way... to get you to come back through again as you were in Syracuse," I say, "I do not want to manipulate you... but just reach you."

Catie says with a sincere look on her face, "I am touched."

I say, knowing that true Catie has been reached, "By the power of God and Christ, leave her, Mombi. Through God and Christ's help, drive her out, Catie! Drive her out! Fight her!"

Catie uses her right arm to grab her left hand, which Mombi has been using to point the wand toward me. They struggle for a while.

Sue Eng Ma Shing continues to spit out black robes with red symbols on her own. Pointing my Cowardly Lion staff at her, I free this Powder of Life creature from her enslavement, and she thanks me from afar.

The Society of the Walking Cane members begin collecting more eggs from the barn to combine with more cloned yo-yos to go with the ones outside. They know the combination spell and simply replicate my idea to prepare more egg-yos for the coming Nomes.

I have telepathically communicated from the Cowardly Lion staff, using E.T.S. (emergency telegraphic service), to Jeremiah Strongs III incognito as the tall hag outside, where he has been waiting in the dark.

The struggle continues between Catie and the spirit of Mombi. Catie has almost wrestled the wand out of her own left hand, which Mombi has been controlling.

Suddenly, from the darkness behind me, comes a tall hag with a green mumbling face all too familiar to me.

Mombi, through Catie, sees the tall green-faced hag and yells, "Just what I need... a strong wicked witch to control, not an Out World brat like you!"

I continue to hit the body of Catie more with holy wine-soaked corks through my own cork gun and shoot pure white light toward her body with the Cowardly Lion staff. Catie continues to fight Mombi over the magic wand. Mombi has been thinking of leaving anyway after she has seen the faux hag behind me and leaves Catie's body.

We watch as a smudgy black spirit leaves Catie, and she collapses to the ground crying. I rush to console Catie. I yell for the Society of the Walking Cane members to put their eggs or even created egg-yos down in the poultry barn and be at the ready. I also whisper to a few other members, including the schoolteacher one, to teleport to meet the festival goers who are coming for the "egg-yo event."

Mombi seems to think they are putting down their egg-yos because they are afraid of who she is entering.

Mombi screams a piercing scream through the ether, "Oh, yes! A proper, strong wicked witch for me to use and control the Nomes with when they arrive! The weak die forever and feel it in hell, and I still live away from it! They should be afraid, those weak wicked wizards and witches who died!" She has a kind of screeching, muffled voice from her smudgy black spirit as if from a bad tape recording or air leaked through the mouthpiece of a stretched balloon. Her voice is loud and piercing yet strained at the same time. It grates the nerves and raises the hairs on the arms.

By the way, the Society of the Walking Cane members do look somewhat frail at times, like a group of Out World senior citizens. Yet as I have stated before, they are very strong, and they have a youthful appearance in their faces and eyes from clean, good living.

They prepare with their staffs but do not put them before them because they do not want to tip Mombi off. Gnarled fingers white-knuckle staffs hidden under the sides of robes.

Soon, Mombi enters the green clay hag face jug, which still does magic mumbling. The R.U.S.E. has thrown a strong alto-esque hag voice for it and it says, "So glad you could join me, Mombi!"

Upon entering the green clay hag face jug, though, the spirit of Mombi realizes something is wrong. I did make the green clay hag face jug appear completely malleable, like flesh while I made it talk. However, it returns to its solid, stiff form once the spirit of Mombi enters it.

She screams, "I'VE BEEN TRICKED! CURSE YOU, DESCENDANT OF DIGGS! I'VE BEEN TRAPPED!"

"I already have been cursed," I state, "And I have been dealing with it all my life. With this, I point my Cowardly Lion staff toward the green face-jug. The Society of the Walking Cane members point their staffs toward the floor of the barn, and a very dark, completely lightless chasm opens up there.

Jeremiah Strongs III removes his Headless Horseman disguise. He holds the green face-jug before him which he had been donning as a faux head. The Society of the Walking Cane strengthens the hold the face-jug has on the evil spirit of Mombi with their staffs.

Mombi yells in a staticky yet echoing, hollow sounding way from inside the green hag face jug,

"I've been summoned back before! I've been summoned from the very edge of hell!"

"How about the deepest part of hell for your being a traitor, black magic user, murderer, abuser, and true kidnapper! –Never, like, been there before, have you?" asked Jeremiah wryly stroking his beard.

He and the Society of the Walking Cane members, along with me, point our staffs out to the carnival horses.

A carnival horse, dark as midnight, dark as Death's horse itself, gallops in, snorts and neighs, and scoops up the green hag face jug by a handle ear with its teeth. The Society of the Walking Cane members had plenty of practice opening up the chasm earlier.

With a gigantic leap, the ebony carnival horse jumps straight down the dark, lightless chasm with the green hag face-jug with Mombi's spirit trapped in like a genii lamp, and we hear the spirit of Mombi yelling as the hag jug breaks at the bottom of the chasm and releases her soul into a place of complete isolation and eternal pain. We hear Mombi's hag voice screaming at the highest and loudest register, "THE AGONY! THE UTTER ALONENESS! AAAAAAAAAAAGH! REVENGE! REVEEEENGE!"

"We can never get our true revenge, but... you will do as an object of it" says a garbled, deep condescending voice.

And with this, not wanting to hear more, the Society of the Walking Cane seals up the chasm, knowing that the faux Death's horse or perhaps true Death's horse from the carnival (who knows?) will make its way back to Death or where it wishes as it's enchanted regardless. Mombi, however, will stay forever in the deepest, solitary darkness with burning sensations, wormy itching, and goblins and demons tormenting her for eternity. Her unremorseful tormenting has returned to her a thousand-fold or more. The Society of the Walking Cane turn their backs for when the chasm closes. They do not want to hear the horrible, last noises.

We all breathe a sigh of relief, and I magick, where I have been tending to Catie, some water for her to drink after the ordeal, hugging her and thanking her for turning to good. She clutches the yellow bricks to her body just as she clutched the toys her father bought her before he abandoned her.

We remain on our toes, though, because we know that Ruggedo and his Nomes as well as the Outworldians being asked to arrive at 6 will arrive at the fair-grounds soon. The schoolteacher, Locasta VII, with the long disciplinary cane staff has gone out to meet them as per my earlier orders. I know she will be good with giving instructions. I point my staff out toward the egg-yos on the field just inside the fair gates and remove their keep-away enchantment if she has not already.

Seeing that Catie is okay, all of us teleport out to where the schoolteacher good witch and a few others are to meet the crowd of kids and adults coming from downtown unknowingly to help us fight the Nomes. It was the only way they would understand... unknowingly. I have dealt with people not understanding for far too long. This has to be the way.

A bitter hatred the likes of which I have never seen in Mombi or any others will soon arrive with the much-defeated but ever power hungry Ruggedo the Re-established Nome King leading his Nomes, and we must be prepared.

Chapter 18

Quite the "Ruggedo-ly", Non-Handsome Nome to Deal with

THE NOMES END UP LOOKING DIFFERENT when they arrive. Instead of the onesie, long-john-esque attire they usually wear, they are covered in the black robes with the red symbols they have plucked from the grasses of the fairgrounds from piles of dust of obvious origins. The Nomes' grey, bulbous heads peep from the robes that are over-sized on them. The Nomes have plucked them from dead grass spots where the wicked witches and evil warlocks were destroyed. The now-gone spirit of Mombi's plan was working.

She had hoped to stick around and be their leader through the red-runed robes and make Ruggedo do her bidding. But the part of her plan in which the, to her, expendable wicked witches and evil warlocks would be replaced with Nomes as a back-up worked. Too bad this battle is not covered by the news, and she does not get any reception where she has gone.

The Nomes are armed with pickaxes and rush towards us. Some of them have clubs with jewels on them than can refract and focus spells from Ruggedo. The tyrant only allows that he should do magic unlike Princess Ozma who still lets Glinda and O.Z. Diggs the First do it even under her relatively no magic rule. He uses the Nomes to focus or refocus his magic here and there. The Nomes pause on Ruggedo's order as he strategizes behind them.

Ruggedo is just behind the row of Nomes and strokes his long beard, which descends down to his bulbous gut, in thought for a moment, sizing us up on the battlefield. He leans against a golden staff bejeweled with every jewel known to Nome-dom embedded throughout it. He wears a necklace around his neck with an Asian bamboo cricket box, which moves to and fro as he scratches his beard. Within the cricket box is an Ozian fiddling cricket, a cricket that uses its hind leg as a bow on a fiddle. A Celtic folk tune instead of an Asian one comes out in a tinny, muffled way through the bamboo box. It is the only sound on the battlefield for now.

I remember from a previous magical flashback that Catie Sheeney's father carried a bamboo cane with him before he left for good and that he had played an Irish folk song on a fiddle for Catie in the train station.

"That's the song me' Da' used to play!" Catie states, hearing a small fiddling song from the cricket box. She has run up behind us after we teleported to the battlefield and have prepared. Knowing the ordeal she has gone through, I ask her to leave, but she arms herself with an egg-yo, wanting to prove herself. Ziggy with the R.U.S.E. on his back and the Cowardly Lion are at my sides in the middle of a long row of Society of the Walking Cane members. On either side of us are Out World citizens who we ask to stay just behind us. They end up advancing just beside us anyway as they are so excited after having been explained what they thought were rules of the egg-yo try-outs.

The Outworldians are not used to Ozian rules of engagement during battles, which usually include a lot of formal lining up and organized attacks in the very rare cases that there is war in Oz.

They immediately start hurling out the egg-yos toward the Nomes. Many of the Nomes scream in high-pitched yet gruff voices, "Eggs! DEADLY EGGS!" When the egg-yos hit them and crack, spilling clear, sticky egg white and bright yellow yolk on their faces and bodies, the Nomes turn to a stone greyer than their skin. Then, the statues that they become disintegrate to dust. Some of the Nomes who are not hit retaliate by going after the Outworldians, but the Society of the Walking Cane members blast them with their staffs (we explain this away as being holographic special effects). Just like the wicked witches and evil warlocks who came before them, all that is left of quite a few of the Nomes now is leather coats with hateful symbols.

The Cowardly Lion starts slashing and jumping on Nomes, eventually turning them to dust and evading their clubs.

Ziggy pushes his way forward and trips Nomes with his shield snout, circling them to go in and trip them. He does not want the reputation of a little ankle biter so does not bite them there. He bruises plenty of ankles, though, and even jumps up to bruise shins, causing many Nomes to fall. If they get hit with the prismatic diamond tip of his elven silver snout-shield, they crumble to dust instantly.

Meanwhile, the Outworldians continue to hurl their egg-yos, the ones I created by cloning Catie's Oz souvenir yo-yo and combining it with two eggs and then reproducing that design, at the Nomes, destroying many along the way. When the eggs crack in the design and are completely re-used, I yell for the Society of the Walking Cane member to produce more.

Ruggedo, who I will never state is King, yells, looking at me with cold flint eyes, "So you have decided to fight dirty with filthy eggs! Just like your father did and look what happened to him!"

I wince at the statement as Dad is still recovering from the magic-induced dementia. He is mostly better now. Thank Lurline.

Before I can react with my Cowardly Lion staff, Ruggedo lifts his golden staff and shoots a red beam from it which is magnified and refracted through the bejeweled clubs the Nomes before him are carrying and concentrated in my direction.

Ziggy leaps up before I can stop him and takes the full force of the beam on the prismatic diamond part of his silver snout shield. The elven runes for valor glow even brighter on his silver dog tag, and the ones for anxiety lessen. The prismatic diamond from the elves on Ziggy's snout-shield shoots the beam back through the clubs the so-called lesser Nomes are carrying. The red beam is reflected and re-concentrated back through the clubs toward Ruggedo.

The red beam has hit Ziggy square on the prismatic diamond nose plate of his armor. However, it is also so powerful that it extends a little to his torso. The magic of the beam makes Ziggy disappear and possibly destroys him! Ziggy is nowhere to be seen or found. The only sound at first nearby is the clang of his armor as it hits the ground. I then cry out and weep. "No-no-no-no-no" I say in repetitive sequence. I weep for a few moments as do the others, but we feel we have to continue fighting.

"No words for this. No words for this!" yells the R.U.S.E. in a squeaky voice over the loss of our friend. The R.U.S.E. was protected by the box I made for him on Ziggy's back some time back.

We do not have to fight for much longer. Ruggedo's magic turns whatever person or creature it comes across into an object that makes sense given what said person is. Hoisted by his own magic petard and thanks to elven magic and Ziggy's valor, Ruggedo's magic is refracted and reflected back to him via Ziggy's prismatic snout cover and Ziggy's past advancement. Ruggedo turns into an object. This is thanks to his own refracted and reflected spell. Ruggedo is now a golden Buddha-like statue with his arms crossed and his legs folded because he felt himself above everybody and always wanted to be unjustifiably basically worshipped. His beard entwines his upper torso a little and then juts out. His face has a permanent scowl behind his now stiff golden yet wildly styled hair. The statue of Ruggedo's bulbous belly juts out even further in his criss-crossed crouching position, but I would not dare rub it for good luck. Embedded within golden Ruggedo statue are jewels of all varieties from diamonds to sapphires to emeralds among others. His golden staff was destroyed when the red blast came back to it.

The refocused magic has had an opposite effect on the little bamboo box with the so-we-thought Ozian fiddling cricket inside it. The so-we-thought Ozian cricket has turned into a human!

It's Mr. Sheeney! He has not aged because of being in Oz all of these years away from his Out World wife and daughter, but the slightly less portly Mr. Sheeney rushes over with his bamboo cane which the bamboo cricket box turned back into.

"We thought you'd died," yells Jeremiah Strongs III and rejoices with laughter.

His schoolteacher good witch friend laughs as well as does his wife Aurora.

"We knew you had that secret mission to go back to Oz and go after Ruggedo years ago," she says, "We thought he had destroyed you completely!"

Mr. Sheeney rushes to hug Catie who weeps profusely and understands without saying anything. We all do. Their hug is the longest and tightest hug I think I have ever seen.

Mr. Sheeney, Catie, and I then both point to the Nomes the others are battling. I wipe tears out of my eyes as does the Cowardly Lion as we continue our battle. As aforementioned, the R.U.S.E. has been left behind in his protective case. The red beam did not reach him. He weeps some slimy tears as well but is careful not to let the tears land on him too much. Salty tears are deadly to the R.U.S.E.

Mr. Sheeney joins his fellow Society of the Walking Cane members with his bamboo cane. He shoots the most tranquil blue beams from it and waits to explain himself more to Catie. Yet given the look on her face, the calm, satisfied look on her face, I know she understands. I also know she will grow to value people over things more and more now.

Seeing their liege turned into the golden idol, those in the Nome Army who have traveled to the Out World, retreat. They have left others back in Oz with other wicked witches and evil warlocks who are still, I am sure, giving my ancestor and Ozma fits. I grab up the Ruggedo golden idol and thrust it into my bag. I also rescue the Powder of Life creature Sue Eng Ma Shing and place her gingerly, wrapped in some cloth, in my bag as well.

The Nomes cannot retreat to the tunnel they have have dug out here through magic, though, because the Society of the Walking Cane blasts many of them as do I, the Cowardly Lion stomps on many of them, and the Out World citizens destroy them with egg-yos. By the time we are done, not a single Nome from the conquering part of the Nome Army of Oz is left in Ionia.

We escort the Outworldians to their cars and thank them for coming to the two-hour demonstration of the egg-yos. They leave with many exciting stories to tell their families about this amazing event.

When we return, Mr. Sheeney is talking to Catie.

He says, in a brogue, "Catie, darlin', I did not mean to leave you for so long as a wee one. I thought I was going to be able to go to Oz and deal with Ruggedo and be back within a week. We had heard he was planning a conquest of the Out World years ago but then the spirit of Mombi starting interfering too. Anyway, Ruggedo had me turned into an object through his magic years before Mombi started her latest plans. But she must have found out about your tragedy somehow and took advantage of it."

"Yes," said Catie, "Yes, she did Da'. Oh... it will be so nice to have ye' ho'oome. I understood the moment I saw you what had happened. I forgive ye. It could not be helped." Some of her brogue was coming back too.

I ask Catie and Mr. Sheeney if they want to travel with me back to Oz.

Mr. Sheeney says, "No... I missed the death of me' dear Out World wife here, and Ruggedo's evil magic kept me away from her and made her heart grow bitter for many a 'year. I t'ink I better go back to Syracuse with me' dear Catie."

Catie hugs him again. She says, "I've been collecting Oz for so many years, wanting to grab a

198

hold of it in so many ways. I don't think I need to go now. When I was latching on to the Oz things my father left me with, what I was really doing was trying to latch on to him."

We all nod.

Catie says, more warmth in her voice than ever before, "Well, now I have him, and he has me, and for the first time in my life, I can honestly say I don't need Oz."

I am taken aback at this as are the others.

I do say, "I am very proud of you, Catie. You have been through a lot and have helped drive evil away from you. That is no small feat!"

I need to start packing to go to Oz, though. Oz still needs me. Some of the contents of the bag I have been carrying have been scattered everywhere, and a bag of dogfood, some bowls, some provisions, and other things are here and there. I pick the things up and notice an open copy of the graphic novel, Ziggy Zig-zags the Light and Dark Fantastic. There in one of the panels is Ziggy winking at me! The graphic novel-created version of Ziggy has returned to the graphic novel itself. Legoohoos, the elf in Elfaw House, was right. He had foreseen all of this. He had stated it would be important that the magically-created Ziggy not be the so-called real version of Ziggy, and I can see why now after the battle with Ruggedo and its result.

"Ziggy's alive!" I yell, "Ziggy's alive and back in the graphic novel where he began!" I show everybody around me. The Cowardly Lion roars a rejoicing roar. The R.U.S.E. squeaks with glee. The still-frame winking Ziggy warms my heart, and I vow to visit the real Ziggy one day. I hear he has visited Oz, after all.

As per the R.U.S.E, he opts to be teleported back to Chittenango Falls in Chittenango, New York among his similar brethren should he ever be needed for translation purposes again. He will not be needed in Oz where all animals can be understood, and most humans and Powder of Life creatures speak the same language despite having some silliness one time to the contrary.

I thank the R.U.S.E. profusely for his service before he is teleported.

The Cowardly Lion states, "For one quite small, much like the Field Mice, you can be very brave. It has been a pleasure to battle alongside you and cannot thank you enough for making me understood in this strange place. I am sure Ziggy would thank you too if he were here."

"Happy to be of service," says the R.U.S.E. and turns to me saying, "I have been among the sophisticated, my friend, and you, Sir, by the way, are no rube." I thank him and wet my hands with a water bottle and gentle pat the R.U.S.E. with a finger. He smiles, raises a slimy neck, waves a stubby, slimy hand, and is teleported away. "RUS-E [phonics] HOME!" he says as he leaves. (There is something very familiar about that yet different.) I smile and cry a little more at the same time that I will no longer see my friend.

I quickly regroup. My long-lost ancestor is there in Oz, though. He had to go back long after the balloon trip back to the Out World. He needs our help, the Ozians, the Society of the Walking Cane, of which I now feel like the most junior-junior member. He needs me and with the loss of my relatives except for Dad through the years, I need him.

I tell the Society of the Walking Cane members that I need for us to teleport to Boone to pick up Dad and have him bring his old hickory stick carved with bears (so much has happened... I didn't mention that). Now that Dad has recovered more from his temporary dementia, more of a kind of magically induced amnesia from Ruggedo, I am going to have Dad bring along his staff and himself with me this time. And we are going to the place we have always dreamed of, have always wanted to help make right after the stories that were passed down to us, and always wanted to be in forever... the true Land of Oz.

Chapter 19
The Final Battle of Oz

WE MAKE QUICK WORK OF THE NOMES IN their underground cavern back to Oz. A few of them escape and retreat to Kaliko to re-establish him as a more benevolent king of the Nomes to replace Ruggedo again.

Wicked witches and evil warlocks dressed in red-symbol-decorated black robes guard the Oz end of the tunnel and keep O.Z. Diggs the First away from it zap us immediately with their wands, but we dodge their fire as we reach the entrance.

The Cowardly Lion charges up and knocks a few of the wicked witches and wizards down.

The Society of the Walking Cane members zap some members of the Society of the Stitches and knock a few of them down. The stitched robe folks are legion near the entranceway, though, and it is all O.Z. Diggs the First can do with a magic force-field to keep them from killing him. My elephant friend and the robotic army of Oz are fending them off as well.

Dad remembers his magic and knocks some of the evil ones down with the black bear force of it from his staff.

The Cowardly Lion, having charged through, swipes and jumps on the evil ones as they try to get closer and closer to O.Z. Diggs and break through his force field.

Jeremiah Strongs the III scribbles over several evil ones with chalk from the end of his staff and makes them disappear in a cloud of chalk-dust. His wife Aurora uses a kind of pussy willow staff with her dragonfly familiar on top to beam out magic as well.

His school teacher friend, who I eventually learn is named Locasta like her ancestor, whacks many of the evil ones away with her disciplinary cane-like staff.

I can get peeps of the outside and how the evil ones are treating my ancestor, at their bloodlust.

Rage enters me. The Cowardly Lion headed staff, though having gone through the trials of the elementals, though having been blessed by God, still reacts to my fallibility at times. I know that I cannot immediately get through to the evil ones. I glare at them in anger.

My rainbow locks are sweaty. My breathing is heavy. Dark, sweaty circles form around the outer edges of my wizard jacket. At times, the evil ones look from my ancestor back to me, confused as to whom is whom, but they realize I am the younger one, despite my ancestor not aging past 50. (If he took his hat off, they would have seen his balding head with the curly pointy tufts on the sides and ended this confusion earlier here at this very moment.)

The Cowardly Lion staff eyes begin to glow red.

Jeremiah says, "No, O.Z., don't do it, no."

"No, son," says my father, looking at me with big hazel eyes, "No... no don't. Do not give in to the hatred. I am angry too. Release it. Release it." I do not listen. My face begins to turn a reddish purple.

A wicked witch points to it and says, "He is going to use magic out of anger! He is going to get closer to becoming one of us!"

I could use what she has stated as a warning, but I do not listen. Her words could have unintentionally turned me against what I was doing but to no avail.

The glowing red in the Cowardly Lion staff head intensifies. Energy builds. I point the staff and BLAM!

30 evil ones are destroyed instantly, and their red-stitched leather robes are left behind.

I snatch one up as a trophy in my rage and thrust it on.

The wicked witches who are left cackle as do the evil warlocks.

The red symbols on the leather jacket begin to, through my mind, tell me to hate my own ancestor, to hate myself.

I start to listen to them and head toward my ancestor's force-field.

I think, 'He is the one responsible for you never being here. He is the one who kept you from being able to come to this great land.'

'He got us all cursed. He is the one who added to our miseries through the years' I add in my vile thoughts. I was already a little angry at my ancestor for some of this. The wickedly enchanted leather jacket with the red hate symbol stitches encourages this rage.

I head toward the force field to destroy it, and suddenly, the collective members of the Society of the Walking Cane shoot beams of calming blue toward me and pull the jacket off of me.

This has thrown the Society of the Stitches off for a while, and I am able to with righteous indignation instead of hate blast them more and more of them away from the force field, helping the Cowardly Lion. I do this while I openly weep.

I think later how close I was to becoming completely evil through my anger but focus at the moment on the task at hand. My ancestor never speaks of it to me. He knows all is well.

Every member of the Society of the Stitches jackets are soon turned to dust from the Society of the Walking Canes' blasts. And I fall to the ground weeping and keening.

My father hugs me, our ancestor's force field descends, and O.Z. Diggs the First rushes to us and says, "I am O.Z. Diggs the First and the Great and Terrible. It feels great to say that again! You need not introduce yourselves, family." O.Z. Diggs the First gives us a hug that encompasses us both and states, "Your grandmother, Madame Staffia, awaits with a feast along with Princess Ozma and all of Oz... only it will be at my castle near Wogglebug U. instead of the Emerald City, which we will visit later after catching up. Come on. Let's travel my favorite way to travel second to balloon!" With this, he waves his own staff with a golden O and Z on the top of it, and we are all whisked away to a banquet table at the wizard-tower donned castle of O.Z. Diggs the First.

Chapter 20

The Non-Prodigal Great-Great-Great and Great Times Four Grandson's Return

VEGETARIAN DISHES OF ALL OF THE MULTI-colored fruits and vegetables and tofu-like transplanted lunch-pail fruit meats of the blue Munchkin Country, green Emerald City, red Quadling Country, yellow Winkie Country, and purple Gillikin Country don the huge banquet table that extends the entire length of the wizard's banquet hall along with goblets of green punch. The banquet hall is decorated in some green items to remind the wizard of his time in the Emerald City but also has some folksy Nebraskan and Kansas touches such as quilts and some musical instruments thanks to the Zoian Madame Staffia.

Sue Eng Ma Shing, of her own volition and joy, is making emerald green monograms on all of the cloth napkins for the guests. The Tin Woodman rewards her with some sewing machine oil, which she states makes her so happy that she wants to "bobbins for apple patterns." She is able to monogram napkins for each of the guests within seconds, and some servants carry the napkins to the table quickly.

Sitting at the banquet hall table beside the seats of honor for the Society members, Cowardly Lion, as well as seats for Princess Ozma and O.Z. Diggs the First at the head of the table, are the Scarecrow, Tin Woodman, Boq, Button Bright, Ugu, Cap'n Bill, Locasta, Glinda, and just too many Ozians to mention.

After we eat the grand meal and wipe our mouths with Sue Eng Ma Shing's wonderful monogrammed napkins, O.Z. Diggs the First states, "We are so grateful to the heroes here, and we hope that they will consider staying in Oz."

Princess Ozma states, "There are plenty of accommodations in the Emerald City and even our various countries for each of you to live here. Many of the Society members' homes remain the way they left them when they left Oz. I saw to that."

The Society of the Walking Cane members each thank her in kind as does my father and me.

O.Z. Diggs states, "It should be noted that through magic that the Society members, including my own relatives, helped us all." He is dressed in his top-hat, his green jacket, and his glasses. He has his Cowardly Lion staff back which he leans on and has given me another oak staff with a Corgi head on it. I gave him back all of his original clothes. I am dressed in a white robe that I make sure is as much like a traditional wizard as possible and nothing at all like a K.K.K. member's. My father is dressed the same way. On my white robe, I wear my O and Z button from back home. My father wears a Land of Oz necklace.

"Here here," says Madame Staffia, who we gave gigantic hugs to before the meal and caught up

207

with some too, "Were it not for Oscar being able to do magic, I do not know what we would have done at times."

Princess Ozma gives it some thought and states, "I hereby amend my decree that only the Wizard, Glinda, and I may do magic in Oz. Those carefully screened members of the Society of the Walking Cane, those benevolent members, may now do magic as they stay in Oz."

I am very happy that my Dad and I will be able to do magic in Oz.

My father whispers to me something I have been thinking.

I stand up and thank everybody for their hard work in the battle and thank Princess Ozma and my ancestor.

I then state, "My father and I would like to stay in this castle with our ancestor and stay in Oz forever. I personally would like to return to the Out World Oz festival as a storyteller to continue to tell the new and old tales I hear here. But I think my father would like to stay behind for more magic practice and a long respite."

"Certainly. Certainly. You're family," said O.Z. Diggs the First. "Your grandmother and I have so much that we want to share with you, stories you may have seen written down by Mr. Baum but so much more!"

We all propose toasts to each other, and I sit back content.

I stare out the window of the wizard castle on the hill and can see the Emerald City green spires off in the distance much like I could see my cabin (which will be transported here soon by the way). I stare out the window at the green spires much like I did the watermill, that Don Quixotic replacement for the windmill back in Boone. My impossible dream has become a reality just as my past reality now seems like a nearly impossible, incomparable dream.

Before I forget, though, pointing to Billina the Hen who is eating some chicken feed at the table along with her chicks, I pull out the golden idol of the Nome King Ruggedo.

"Princess Ozma," I state, "Might I suggest before we get embroiled in another adventure way too soon after this long one, that we do something?"

"Certainly," states Princess Ozma, flinging back her black locks beneath her O and Z crown with the side, dried poppies, "Anything within reason... anything within reason according to Oz and pleasing to Fairy Queen Lurline and myself."

I state, still pointing at the lovely, talking hen, "Make water troughs to keep witches away and square off Billena's chicken coop and near her nest and eggs may this golden idol of the former King Ruggedo, former King of the Nomes, go forever."

I pull out the golden idol of Ruggedo with the jewels, and everyone at the long banquet table applauds and gasps.

"I think I know why," states Ozma, smiling, "But for the benefit of the others, please explain."

"There may be a wicked witch we have not seen or a warlock too. The water will keep the witches away. You can enchant the coop too to further keep warlocks and witches away. To make absolutely sure no Nomes try to retrieve the idol, I suggest putting it right by Billena's eggs."

"Well, Billena," asks Princess Ozma of the hen.

Billena clucks, "I, bock, do not mind the golden idol being there. I am going to cover it up, though, in case my chickadees turn into idol-worshipping savages, though."

I joke, "Might I suggest not covering it up with any leather etched in red stitches."

"Please do not," laughs my father, his grey beard cavorting.

O.Z. Diggs the First exclaims, "I have just the thing!"

He rushes up his wizard tower in a huff and rushes back down on clicking black boot heels.

Before him he has a silken package with different primary colored squares showing on it.

"Cover it up with my old balloon silks," says O.Z. Diggs, "I won't be needing those ever again. I plan on staying here forever... with my family." O.Z. Diggs hands the balloon silks to one of Princess Ozma's attendants, Jellia Jamb or somebody comparable.

"I've still got quite a few Out World adventures left in me as storyteller too," I add, "But I certainly will not be traveling by balloon either... probably just through magic."

Soon after, the banquet festivities die down, and I ask in the morning after we rest if we can find a place for Sue Eng Ma Shing to live if she does not want to live in the castle. I want her as a Power of Life creature to have a choice of where she wants to go. I want her to have freedom.

Sue Eng Ma Shing states, "You may not have noticed my vibrant pink color before. I was designed to be a beginner sewing machine marketed for young ladies. (We know guys can sew too...that is how old the machine she was created from was.) What I most want to do is what I heard from Catie that I used to do... I think I used to do this for her Oz dolls... I want to make clothes for dolls!"

O.Z. Diggs the First says, "Well, it just so happens there happens to be a sub-country of dolls within Oz. We will go there tomorrow and take a grand tour on the way, stopping by the Emerald City and seeing all of the sights."

Sue does some r-r-r-rr's of excitement, and Dad and I are very excited about the tour as well.

The meat creatures, what non-Powder of Life creatures, are called begin to yawn. We decide to go to bed and go on this mini-adventure in the morning.

After our mini-adventure to the Country of the Baby-dolls, our first of many, our ancestor, great-great-great-great grandmother, my father, and I retire to the green-decorated parlor back at O.Z. Diggs the First's castle, replete with peacock feathers and peacock décor thanks to Grandma Madame Staffia.

And with much shared love, the stories we share and tell are at once some of the most unreal and real I have ever heard or told. This is definitely an end that will serve as a new beginning in the wonderful Land of Oz...

About the Author

Ron Baxley, Jr., a native of the small Southern town of Barnwell, South Carolina, lived in the state's urban areas as well as Massachusetts for two years.

He has been a published author for 26 years since he had a skit published in a glossy youth magazine. A graduate from the University of South Carolina-Aiken with a B.A. in English in 1998, Ron wrote essays and a column for the "The Baum Bugle," the journal of the International Wizard of Oz Club and wrote an Oz book, *The Talking City of Oz*, published by the late Oz author March Laumer's "The Vanitas Press" in 1999. Ron later added to it and released it as a self-published Second Edition with illustrations by Gwendolyn Tennille in 2010.

Before and shortly after the new millennium, Ron, an avid life-long reader of various genres, had poems, stories, articles, and essays published in "Nostalgia", "Filmfax", "Parsec", "The Rambler", and other literary sources. He has also self-published multiple book versions of satirical science fiction.

Ron received attention for his Oz book in 2010 at Oz-Stravaganza, a festival in Chittenango, New York, the birthplace of L. Frank Baum, and as a result was invited to attend. He has been invited to that festival as a participating author in Authors and Artists Alley nearly every year since and was awarded the "International L. Frank Baum and All Things Oz Lifetime Membership" in 2016 because of his contributions to the literary world of Oz. He co-wrote an Oz/Wonderland "Of Cabbages..." series with James C. Wallace II which was self-published individually and promoted there and then combined and published by the now defunct small press Maple Creek Press. Ron's Oz book, The Oz Omnibus of Talking City Tales which contained three small books that were sequels to his The Talking City of Oz, was published for three years by Maple Creek Press until 2016. Ron has also been a special guest author at the Wizard of Oz Festival-Ionia (now named the Michigan Wizard of Oz Festival for 2018) as well as national cons, and was an authorial vendor at OzCon International in San Diego, California in 2015. He lives with his fur-child, Ziggy, a Pembroke Welsh Corgi, upon whom he based a graphic novel, Ziggy Zig-zags the Light and Dark Fantastic (with illustrations by Vincent Myrand), with a second volume coming soon and combined with the first. Ron also lives with a relative for whom he is a care-giver. He, also having worked in service jobs as a cook, clerk, retail sales-person, book-seller, and "edu-tainer", was an educator for 15 years in various capacities, had worked on his certification early in that process, and is currently a part-time correspondent/reporter with the Orangeburg Times & Democrat (formerly a full-time reporter for The

Aiken Standard"), is a contributing writer for the Disney fan site, DisneyAvenue.com, and is a part-time travel specialist for Mad Hatter Adventures Travel Company, for which he specializes in selling Disney vacations of various types. Ron recently signed a contract with the Choice of Games company for a completed Oz parody adventure game he programmed and wrote entitled "NE by NW OZ". The game, with over 10 illustrations by *USA Today* graphic designer Ian Clyde, should appear in 2018 on the Hosted Games tab on www.choiceofgames.com.

He is currently working on an accepted non-fiction book for another press to be announced at a later date and hopes to release other fiction besides *O.Z. Diggs Himself Out* through YBR Publishing.

O.Z. DIGGS HIMSELF OUT

O.Z. DIGGS HIMSELF OUT

CPSIA information can be obtained
at www.ICGtesting.com
Printed in the USA
LVHW020859310522
720088LV00008B/744

9 780998 058252